COURAGE

MY

LOVE

SARAH DEARING

COURAGE

MY
LOVE

Stoddart

A NOVEL

Published in 2001 by Stoddart Publishing Co. Limited
895 Don Mills Road, 400-2 Park Centre, Toronto, Canada M3C 1W3

Distributed in Canada by:
General Distribution Services Ltd.
325 Humber College Blvd., Toronto, Ontario M9W 7C3
Tel. (416) 213-1919   Fax (416) 213-1917
Email cservice@genpub.com

Distributed in the U.S. by:
General Distribution Services Inc.
PMB 128, 4500 Witmer Estates,
Niagara Falls, New York 14305-1386
Toll-Free Tel. 1-800-805-1083 Toll-Free Fax 1-800-481-6207
Email gdsinc@genpub.com

05 04 03 02 01 1 2 3 4 5

Canadian Cataloguing in Publication Data

Dearing, Sarah
Courage my love

ISBN 0-7737-6210-8

I. Title.

PS8557.E22587C67   2001   C813'.54   C00-932946-3

PR9199.3.D42C67   2001

U.S. Cataloging in Publication data is available
from the Library of Congress

Cover Design: Bill Douglas @ The Bang
Text design: Kinetics Design & Illustration

THE CANADA COUNCIL | LE CONSEIL DES ARTS
FOR THE ARTS | DU CANADA
SINCE 1957 | DEPUIS 1957

*We acknowledge for their financial support of our publishing program the
Canada Council, the Ontario Arts Council, and the Government of Canada
through the Book Publishing Industry Development Program (BPIDP).*

Printed and bound in Canada

For all the freaks who
help keep the beige at bay

*The work of art of the future will
be the construction of a passionate life.*

— RAOUL VANEIGEM,
THE REVOLUTION OF EVERYDAY LIFE

Mrs. Philippa Maria Donahue only wandered into Kensington Market to buy herself a fish, but standing there, right there on Baldwin Street, staring at a shark's entrails, she nearly fainted, not from the smell, which was considerable, nor from the unusual colours and textures spilling out. The entrails gurgled for a moment and spoke to her. In a surprisingly clear and ordinary male voice, they told her: "Leave your husband. Leave him now."

Philippa looked elsewhere for the source of the voice and was completely alone on the street but for the dead thing hanging on a hook before her.

"Why?" she whispered at the fish, which chose to remain silent.

"Why?" she said again, to herself this time, meaning why had she imagined this voice? Schizophrenia can begin with voices. She knew this. She didn't know — wasn't convinced — that she was ready to abandon her marriage.

The heat, too, caused her to feel dizzy, and a particularly noxious Toronto humidity trapped a cloying mixture of pungent fish and garbage odours in the airless street around her. She considered the shark once more, gave it a final opportunity to prove itself, and made a prudent move to a seat on a shaded patio.

A skinny, unsmiling waitress with a ring in her eyebrow and another hidden in her labia took her order. Philippa forgot to gawk at the piercing, but had the labial ring been exposed, it might have held her eye.

Mrs. Philippa Maria Donahue was thirty-one years of age. She had thick black tresses and soft green eyes. "My Irish Princess," her husband often said.

"Ireland has no princesses," she would tell him, as if he were dim. "Only fairies. And goddesses."

She clenched her teeth, thinking of the term of endearment in the context of the shark's enteric message. This led her to recall other aspects of her husband that had been irritating her: simple things such as locking the bathroom door, returning meals in restaurants, forever flossing before bed. His very name, a perfectly lovely Irish name like Brendan, he insisted on shortening to Dan. The rapidity with which the long list of grievances scrolled through her mind startled her, the resulting analysis being that perhaps she was not developing schizophrenia.

Relieved that it was just hatred, or at least boredom, she relaxed and surveyed the activity around her.

A young man, using the pavement as a makeshift shop, was arranging an odd collection of vintage hats and shoes on a striped and moth-eaten Hudson's Bay blanket next door. He occasionally stood back to assess the overall effect created by the slightest shift of a toe. Philippa wondered if he was a tinker, if an itinerant life in a caravan was somehow acceptable here. She closed her eyes for a few moments to think of it: freedom. When she opened them, he was there, sitting directly across from her, shirt removed, skin slightly moist from the heat, staring at her from behind the intimidating lenses of state-trooperish glasses.

He spoke as though the moment had been clipped from a colourized print of an old gangster film, said, "Trouble you for a smoke, darling?"

Philippa pushed her Marlboro package towards the man without speaking. He took four.

"Cheers," he said, and slowly rose, maintaining his gaze. Philippa watched as he scrutinized his display one more time before trotting up the walkway and into the store.

"Come back," she whispered. "I need to talk to you."

He emerged fifteen minutes later and appeared not to remember her. Philippa continued to study him. Every movement seemed precisely choreographed for effect, at the same time being perfectly fluid and natural, not affected in the least, the way some people's are. Though she was certain he could sense her staring, he never acknowledged it. She felt oddly connected to him and slightly nauseated, infected with a sudden and totally irrational desire to watch him for the rest of her life.

People on the street stopped, or were stopped, and he attempted to sell them mismatched shoes, claiming the word in Paris was "hot." A few of the women were fooled, convinced, perhaps, by his intensity, or a need to be first in on a trend, and tried on the suggested combination. Finally someone bought a hat, and with his new wealth he came to a table on the patio.

He positioned himself in the sun, ordered a beer, and turned to face Philippa. She thought he was about to speak and her mouth went dry as his lips parted slightly, but it was only to allow his tongue, barely visible, to lick softly at the side of his mouth and withdraw. Moments later the tip reappeared between his teeth and they slowly compressed. Philippa knew the pressure of them on her own tongue, then realized she too was biting into flesh. She felt her nipples harden and push against her tee-shirt so violently that she looked to see whether they'd actually pierced it. She imagined the tongue on them, the teeth. He removed his aviator glasses, and one blue eye, partnered by brown, locked her own in a visual embrace. The eyes shifted downwards then, met hers in recognition, and moved slowly along her neck, breasts, belly. They rested on her crotch, causing her to shift slightly, and her legs relaxed, sundered to allow his stare to penetrate her. She leaned back to feel the sun and, even with her eyes closed, felt only his wet heat probing every crevice of her body as though it were a strong tongue. She opened her eyes and her mouth as she experienced her first orgasm, opened them in shock at this phenomenon.

He winked the brown eye at her, then vanished like a mirage.

Philippa ordered another beer to cool herself down, and found a phone in the basement, occupied by what might have been a woman — though she couldn't be certain — screaming about where the fuck someone was with the shit.

She didn't wait long, and his familiar, too-loud voice brought her back into her body.

"Hi, princess. What's up?"

"I'm going home for a few days. Clear my head, see the folks."

"Good idea. I have to work all weekend anyway, wouldn't be much fun."

Philippa grimaced at the obvious. "No," she agreed, he wouldn't.

◆

That Friday afternoon, armed with the conviction of loathing and a renewed awareness of life's sensual possibilities, Mrs. Philippa Maria Donahue dissolved herself in the atmosphere. She bought an assortment of second-hand clothes from a store called Exodus, a "fill a bag" sale that supplied her with a small but charming wardrobe for twenty-five dollars. She instinctively knew what she would do, and for the first time in her adult life, set aside her carefully cultivated tastes and values. Rather than live by her established rules of conduct, good manners, and good breeding, her reconstruction chose only physical boundaries to rule her life. Had she been a dog, or a man for that matter, she would have marked her territory with her scent, thought to in fact, but discarded the idea as unnecessary and excessive. She staked her territory by walking along its edges, drew a line around her life as she did so, using the streetcar tracks as a physical reference: Spadina Avenue and its mobbed Chinatown at the east, across a barren stretch of College to Bathurst, south at a place called Sneaky Dee's and back along Dundas Street, past a hospital and swimming pool and tenement housing. Insulated, in her mind, from the rest of the world, the final act of her former self was to inform her parents. The telephone wouldn't do for the blunt pronouncement she desired to make, and the O'Sheas had not embraced the information superhighway, so Philippa sent an old-fashioned wire from a mysterious and archaic shop in Chinatown, thinking it romantic, and in any event simpler.

Ma, Da,
I think I've left Brendan today, though he doesn't quite know it yet. You may hear from him. Don't worry, I'm well. I just needed to escape before I became too much the wife. I'm too young for that.

Love you both.
Phillie

◆

Mrs. O'Shea laughed when she received the telegram, knowing too well herself the wearying aspects of being a wife. Mr. O'Shea blamed her personally.

"She's inherited the tinker in you."

"Yes, Liam, I suppose she has. You cannot fault me for it."

"Of course I can fault you for it. Nothing else can explain it."

"She's likely just bored. Dan is an awful bore."

"She should have considered that before she married the lad and moved to that country up there."

"Well, she didn't want to go. Couldn't you tell?"

"I thought it was the other thing."

There was no point arguing, and she waved away his contrarity with a flip of her backhand.

"D'you suppose we should ring him?"

"I want no part in it." Liam O'Shea squinted at his wife of thirty-two years. "You're going to have a good laugh at this one, aren't you Siobhan? You'll be laughing out the other side of your face when the girl gets herself in the soup."

"She won't get in the soup. Phillie's a good girl wit.
head on her shoulders. Tinkers survive. It's in our blood."

"I never should have married one meself."

"Come now, *you* would have been bored with anyone else.
Go on and listen on the other line."

Siobhan dialed her son-in-law and moments later heard
her husband pick up the extension.

"Hello Brendan — Dan — it's Siobhan O'Shea . . . Yes I
know Phillie's not there, we've just received a note from her
. . . No, not a postcard, a telegram of all things, saying she's
fine but needed a break . . . No, not exactly . . . Before I
became too much the wife, it says . . . No Dan . . . No other
word . . . Yes, of course."

Liam O'Shea felt less calm than his wife and broke in at
this point to inform Dan that he held him personally responsible for his daughter's well-being.

"I don't know what's going on up there, what would make
our Phillie do such a thing, but if it's because of something
you've done to her, I'll come up there myself and haul her back
home to Cincinnati where she belongs." With that, he hung
up the phone.

◆

Philippa returned to Kensington Avenue and went into the
store where she hoped to find the tinker for some advice.
Asylum, it was called, painted red, white, and blue in a stars-
and-stripes motif that soothed her, made her feel she was
being wrapped in a protective emblem of her country as she
stepped in. A sign by the cash register advertised a room for
rent, fifty dollars per week, and a quick inspection revealed a
single bed, a rough wooden chair, and an incongruous mauve
bidet that challenged green ivy wallpaper for dominance over

the space. She thought the bidet charming, thought it might make her feel she was living in a Parisian garret, and paid in advance for a month. There was no linen, but it was stifling anyhow, so she lay on the bare and stained mattress, thinking with satisfaction, if only her husband could see his Irish princess now.

Shouts came through her window and fell into her dream, caused it to shift away from pleasant, so that when she awakened Philippa was afraid, unable to distinguish reality from her dream and believing someone had entered her room. She lay still, willing invisibility, until she heard the noise again, clearly from the street. Several hours must have passed for it to be so dark, and not knowing the time added to her disorientation.

She dressed in her new used clothes, the look stolen from some of the women she'd seen that day. Gap walking shorts and matching taupe tee-shirt were replaced with purple crushed-velvet leggings and a black lace top over vintage brassiere. Philippa Maria Donahue would never wear such things. Her husband would not have approved. The bra was the best, creating a style of voluptuous and pointed tartiness that had always evaded her. So costumed, she entered her new world.

"Whoa, girlie-girl, where do you think you're going?" It was the tinker, sitting alone at Café Kim next door.

"For a walk," she replied with a false air of casualness.

He snickered.

"Let me buy you a beer, doll. You're new around here. There's things you should know before you step out for an evening stroll."

Philippa paused, uncertain of her ground and why this

man was here, apparently waiting for her. She felt safe enough outside, so joined him and immediately thought of an alias to help her slip out of her self.

"Nova Philip," she said, offering her hand.

"Tommy Gunn," he replied, taking it in his, leering slightly at her. "Your parents were some sort of hippies or something, naming you that?"

"It's not my real name." She blushed, suddenly feeling silly, though it wasn't the first time Mrs. Philippa Maria Donahue had renamed herself.

"No shit," he said.

"And yours is!" she replied defensively, ignorant of people who really do fit their names, become them, but he told her: "Course. Not only is the name real, I am the name."

"So, have you been waiting for me, Tommy Gunn?"

"Don't flatter yourself, darling. You're hot, but not red hot. I'm simply waiting out another night in the war zone."

Mrs. Philippa Maria Donahue hardly expected such a flat dismissal from this person who had, only a few hours earlier, penetrated her with his eyes. "It's me," she wanted to say. "Hell-ooo . . . don't you remember?"

"What war zone?" she asked instead.

"The war on drugs. As we speak, it's going down. We've got a ringside seat."

She glanced around the deserted street and saw nothing to indicate a war.

"What are you talking about?"

"See that building on the corner? In a couple hours, a hundred special-forces police officers will storm it and take out the biggest crack dealer in the city."

"How do you know?"

"Ears, darling. Also, I tipped off the cops."

"Why?"

"I'm tired of rock heads. They bore me."

"Is it safe to sit here?"

"Fuck no. But it'll blow your mind. I wish I could get my hands on a camcorder. You got one? We could sell the video to one of those eyewitness programs."

Nova shook her head. This was out of her league. He was, quite possibly, out of her league. She felt like an Irish princess and Tommy sensed it. Curbing his enthusiasm for a shootout, he tried to reassure her.

"You're safe with me. I'm just teasing you, trying to let you know what you're in for wandering the streets at night."

"So it's not true?"

"No, baby, it's true."

She chewed on a bit of tough skin around her thumbnail, a nervous habit she'd given up years ago when manicures became a weekly ritual, and picked up now as a comfort.

"I have a room next door," suggested Nova. "Do you want to watch from there?"

"And leave my pint? I don't think so."

She chewed some more as she tried to get a grip on her surroundings, wondered if she was possibly being halfwitted about this, and asked if he believed in sixth sense.

He believed in nine, actually: sight, hearing, taste, touch, smell, danger, safety, direction, precognition.

"But are danger and safety really senses?"

"Sure. Danger causes a reaction to help us survive, so does safety. That's sense. That's their purpose."

"Isn't it simply intuition?"

He shook his head. "Think about it. We're really not so far

removed from the other animals in the jungle. Contrary to popular wisdom, your senses, not your intellect, are the key to survival . . . if you pay proper attention to them."

Nova Philip thought of her earlier desire to mark her territory, her impulsive decision to heed a voice that may or may not have been real. Sitting there in relative darkness, with the wrong kind of stranger, in the wrong sort of neighbourhood, she identified a queasiness more to do with anticipation and titillation than with danger.

"Will they have guns?" she asked.

"Oh yeah," he said matter-of-factly, as he reached for one of her cigarettes.

"So why don't I sense danger? Other than that of my cigarettes disappearing."

He ignored the sideways complaint. "Like I said, you're not in danger. I'll protect you."

Nova considered him an unlikely protector.

"You can't protect me from a bullet," she said.

"Why would anyone want to shoot you?"

"They may well want to shoot you for being a squealer and get me instead."

"If I thought anyone would be shooting at me, would I be out here?"

"Does anyone think they'll be shot at?"

"Some. They're none too bright, though, and walk into it."

"What about the innocent people who get shot?"

"They do stupid things."

"Such as sit outside waiting for wars to begin? Or tipping off the cops?"

"No. Such as walk around at night and maybe enter the wrong address."

The intrusion of an unenthusiastic waitress came as a blessing for Nova, an injection of reality, of a few concrete and normal words into this conversation about being shot at. She ordered a Corona, and the girl curled her lip, in a strangely good-humoured way, at Tommy.

"I observed you today," Nova said quietly when they were alone again. "You seem to know everyone around here."

"It's my business to know."

"Your business?"

"Yeah. It's my hood."

"I thought that was a Black expression."

"No one owns words."

Nova lit a cigarette, used the time out to consider and carefully articulate her own.

"Do you know what you did to me this afternoon?"

"Tell me," he said, challenged her to do so with a lascivious tone.

She had hoped he would simply nod, use one of those additional senses to help *her* survive the moment. He was trying to sully it, might as well have asked her straight up to talk dirty to him. And while she thought that might not be out of the question some time down the road, Nova declined to play at present. Her immediate need was to understand. She described the event as clinically as she could, tried to strip it of erotic undertones. Since they'd already shared such an intimate act — never mind the absence of physical contact — she felt entitled to discuss it openly.

"Just by looking at me, you aroused me."

"How much?"

"Completely."

Tommy Gunn felt entitled to something entirely different.

"I believe you owe me a pint, then," he said.

She supposed she did, and when the waitress returned with her lime-capped bottle, she ordered a second.

"Not that bilge water," he said. "Bring me a pint of Upper Canada Dark."

She immediately thought of gift horses, but caught herself when she considered the source, when she remembered Nova.

"Cheers," he said.

"Slainte," she replied.

"What's that?"

"Gaelic."

"You Irish?"

"Irish American."

"Then you should know all about getting blowed up real good."

"I'm more American than Irish, born and bred in Cincinnati. The Troubles never affected my life directly."

"Ahhh. A genuine Miss Melting Pot. Why'd you leave?"

"I came here for six months with my husband. It turned . . ." She wondered what exactly had turned and where. What was the precise turning point? "Permanent," she said. "It turned permanent."

"So where's he?"

"At home, I guess."

"You guess?"

"He believes I'm away for the weekend. I think I've left him." Verbalized, hearing the words instead of just thinking them, it became more real and very nearly frightening, so she tempered her statement. "I'm not certain of it, though."

"How can you be uncertain about something like that?"

"I may have schizophrenia instead. I heard a voice today. It told me what to do."

"What, God told you to leave your husband?"

"No. Not God, unless you believe He speaks through all creatures, which he might do. A shark. Its organs, really. They spoke to me earlier."

Tommy was able to expressively mock her with a single raised eyebrow, so it was redundant when he said, "Perhaps you're just fucked up."

She shook her head. "That's the crazy thing. I don't feel fucked up in the slightest. It was as though my brain was one of those Etch-a-Sketch boards, suddenly wiped clean of all the scribbles. I was struck by a sudden and strange sense of clarity — a gut feeling, so to speak. I'll wait and see. It's nice to have a break from him at any rate. I was beginning to feel like such a wife."

"How does that feel exactly?"

"An appendage. A bore. Bored."

"Not all wives are appendages. They're not all boring, either."

"No, but for the last little while, I've felt it. I'm not myself. I don't like me very much, no matter what I do to try to fix it."

"That's your problem, doll. Not his fault."

"What a typically male thing to say."

"Why?"

"You have no idea of the role expected, the pressure."

"What big pressure? Deciding what's for dinner? What to wear? Whether to have sex and pretend to like it?"

"That's not fair. And it's very tired."

"I know. So tell me."

Nova didn't believe this cocky presence could comprehend

because she assumed he'd never felt trapped. She gazed rather blankly into the distance as she tried to articulate precisely what it was she was running from.

"I just feel it. I felt a need to escape the entrenchment, like overwhelming anxiety."

"See, I'm right. Join the human race, Nova, and get a real problem."

Nova finished her beer and rose to leave, suppressed the desire to spit in his face.

"Your mood ring's turning black, doll."

"Fuck you!" She stomped down the street, away from the place with the guns, repeated the profanity she seldom uttered to try to restore her resolve. It was *her* thought, *her* anxiety, and real, despite what anyone else might think.

The least-scary bar on the street was called The Last Temptation. Once again the significance was lost to her, but the names in this place were contributing to her state of mind, functioning as subconscious signposts for a new direction. A long-haired, leftover hippie sat at one of the back tables with a guitar, playing for no one. He sang about a woman gone crazy on the street, and since the entire back wall was covered with an image of the one she'd just left, Nova believed his song was being composed on the spot and exclusively for her benefit.

◆

Tommy began to fret. It was what he did best, or most, as self-appointed guardian of Kensington Market. The girl was not ready for the Market, of that he was certain.

He found her at The Temp and seated himself at a table across from her. She tried to ignore him, but he sat, head in hands, ogling her, occasionally sighing and pretending to moon. When his clowning released a tiny laugh, he took it as licence to join her, flourishing a bouquet of fluffy, white hydrangea stolen from a garden. Nova thought it rude to divide her attention and converse during a performance, so kept him shushed until the song was finished. She applauded wildly, while Tommy practised his bored look, and then asked him about the mural.

"It's a piece of shit, really," he said, and tried to brush off the subject.

"I think it's brilliant," she persisted.

"Why's that?"

She thought it was so true, not just physically, but spiritually, somehow portraying the soul of the street.

"You want to leave here and go stand out there, to be part of it," she said.

"I'm sure the owner wouldn't like to know it has *that* effect. It's mine."

"You did that?"

"Yup."

"I'm impressed."

"Don't be. And don't get too close. It loses its magic if you get too close. Like so many things."

"Come now. You're not one of those stereotypical artists who believes nothing they do is good enough."

"It's just the perspective, meant to be most powerful from the door, to draw people in, not drive them out." Tommy helped himself to a gulp of her beer and squinted at his work. "Actually, I quite like it. And there's nothing stereotypical about me."

Nova affirmed this with a nod. There was no denying she was in the company of a true individual, and she felt vaguely threatened by his authenticity and disarmed by her inability to properly peg him. He wasn't even remotely her type, with his longish hair matted into braid-like things, not quite dreadlocks, a big crooked nose, and dirty fingernails. Once she noticed the fingernails, she relaxed a little about how she was being perceived.

"I'm entitled to my opinion," she said. "You're entitled to yours. Let's just leave it at that."

"What entitles you to an opinion on art?" he challenged.

"What gives you the right to judge people so harshly?"

"I'm not judging you. I'm asking a question. Anyway, I hate talking about art. It bores me. I was worried about you."

"You've no need to worry about me. I'm a big girl, about a quarter tinker on my mother's side."

"I guess that's what we have in common then." He put a long and sturdy finger to his lips, rolled his eyes in mock horror, and said, "Big family skeleton."

Mrs. Philippa Maria Donahue appreciated the problematic nature of suspect gene pools, and it helped to explain the attraction, made her feel a little less irrational about it. Cut from the same ragged cloth they were, just in different patterns, sewn up into their current garments by different tailors. His genetic makeup might explain how he was able to enter her with his otherwise lambent eyes.

Because it intrigued her, because she'd never before met a real-life artist and wanted to familiarize herself with how one might actually think, she ignored what caused his boredom and said, "It must be wonderful to be an artist, to have an artist's vision."

"What? Are you loose? It's frustrating as hell, because no one else seems to see things the same way I do."

"And how's that?" She expected an explanation directly related to his iridic inconsistency, those eyes registering differently than her own nicely matched set.

"These flowers," he said, picking up two from the bunch. "What are they to you?"

"I've never seen them before."

"But do they look like anything you've seen?"

"No," she said, without consideration, without employing her imaginative faculties.

He danced the spherical, fluffy blooms like stick puppets along the edge of the table.

"POODLES, perhaps?" He continued the action, trying, for her benefit, to animate the inanimate. "They're poodles to me, plain as day. On stems."

Nova eyed the flowers, couldn't push her imagination fully around the barrier of fact that they were indeed flowers, so he continued his discourse on the mysteries of his composition.

"Pick a word."

"What?"

"Just pick a word and say it."

"Music."

"It's a red word."

He waited for a sign of comprehension, a flicker of appreciation for the hues of language, but was isolated once again.

"All words have a colour association for me," he explained. "When people talk, I get flashes of rainbows."

"How?"

"Fuck if I know. It just happens. Not always, but often, like my senses are all either interconnected or short-circuiting. I'm not sure which."

"Is it some sort of disorder?"

"Dis-order? Depends on how you view order, now don't it? I like to think of it as a highly evolved state of being. It's called synaesthesia."

Nova sighed and confessed she didn't think she truly saw things at all, never mind colours for words. He placed his hand over hers, not exactly holding it. His touch was a contact point for transferring energy and information, for as self-appointed guardian of Kensington Market, Tommy Gunn considered it an essential part of his job to convert people to his way of seeing the place.

"If you stick around the Market and flow with its in-your-face spirit, you'll either begin to see or decide you don't really want to after all. Stuck here, you can't avoid the smells, the noise, the people: some pleasant, others wicked, and some truly orgasmic." He paused to allow Nova to register his self-reverence. "Yeah, yeah, roll your eyes. Like it's ever happened to you before. Like it didn't freak you right out of your underwear."

Nova freed her hand before its sweatiness revealed how freaked she was.

"Anyway," Tommy continued, "you'll have to take the bad with the good, because you'll find them in equal proportions."

"So where do you suggest I go from here?"

"Ever sucked on a piece of sugar cane?"

Nova shook her head at the seemingly tangential query.

"Tried durian? It reeks of rotting flesh, but the taste is dreamy, sweet and custard-like, worth the trial of getting beyond its stench, maybe even because of it. Sample a new food each day. You can get Salvadorean pupusas for two bucks, Vietnamese tofu subs with a whole handful of fresh cilantro for one. After you've eaten their food, you can talk to the people. They have real lives, you know, complex. There are even a few authentic schizophrenics around who would be glad to demonstrate what it's all about." He took another swig from her bottle before continuing. "Just by talking to them, you become part of their lives. I promise, your entire perception of the world will change. You'll start to notice other things, how tired they look, how they carry themselves after a life of bending in rice fields or just spending ten hours on their feet. You'll actually notice the expressions on their faces, and begin to wonder what joy or pain or anger is in their eyes, their lives. Sometimes, you might even find out."

As he concluded, the day's events, the voice, whether of God or not, acquired a concrete meaning she could latch onto, one that didn't sound as flighty as mere marital dissatisfaction or fear of stasis. And it was true. Mrs. Philippa Maria Donahue had for too long viewed people casually encountered as little more than a steady stream of moving objects to tolerate or avoid. She'd isolated herself from the real world around her, closed it off to keep at a safe and blissful distance.

"Will you help me?" she asked, sincere, slightly embarrassed, and unusually shy.

"When I have the time."

Nova pouted unintentionally but thoroughly, a perfectly adolescent petulance certain women can get away with, the kind of wounded-sparrow look some men find irresistible. Tommy Gunn could resist the look, but not the opportunity to play guru for this new entry into his territory.

"Don't do that. God, I hate that. I'll show you. But don't be thinking I can take care of you. I can barely take care of myself. I'll point you in a few right directions, steer you from the wrong ones. Okay?"

"Okay," she smiled.

"Come by the Plate tomorrow at noon. I'll introduce you to some people, and then I'm putting on a little performance across the street."

He was not a person to sit still for very long, and had a cop show to watch besides. He convinced her to return to her room, despite not being sleepy. Their conversation had revved up her mind, and she lay awake in the darkness, listened for the war to begin, and stared at white blobs of petals that still looked like flowers, though she tried harder this time.

An inconsiderate motorist woke her at 8 AM with an obnoxious push on his horn. Given that Philippa Maria Donahue was a nine-hour kind of woman when it came to sleep, the robbery of two of them, on a day when she could least afford the loss, was a significant crime against her humanity. Sleep theft may not be tangible, not yet proven in court, but Philippa thought it should be punishable for the loss of something irreplaceable or the diminished quality of a day. When the noise rankled her a second time, longer, excessive, beyond rude, she got up quickly, leaned out the window, and suggested the driver relax and show just a little regard for people sleeping.

He stared up at the figure of Nova, positioned like a carved siren at the prow of an ancient ship, and without a reasonable response to the sight of a naked woman during Saturday morning chores, blasted his horn once again at a delivery van blocking the progress of his shiny new mini model.

"Eejit," Nova muttered, and as she withdrew, realized her unclothed status. She pressed herself against the wall beside the window, looked around the room for her robe, and remembered she didn't have it with her. A plastic bag of clothes lay in the corner, and seeing it helped her recover from the cognitive dissonance common to people who awaken with a start in a strange room, deprived of adequate sleepy time. She crawled under the window and rummaged through the contents: one athletic stripe tee, a pair of frayed denim shorts, a bowling shirt with the name "Stan" embroidered on the pocket, and an over-dyed full slip.

She'd once owned a cocktail dress designed to resemble a slip and assumed the real thing would be as good as the imitation, but without the ironic accessories — army boots or running shoes — she was an oblivious "Glamour Don't." Without tattoos and attitude and holey fishnets, hers was a look of madness, but with no mirror to consult in her fifty-dollar room, too few options, and too little sleep, she left the house in her underwear.

◆

It was a pig of a day: filthy, sweaty, and fat. With high humidex and UV ratings at such an early hour, she felt a primal urge to roll around in cool mud and stay thus covered, protected, and temperate. It had rained during the night so the pavement steamed up little knee-high whorls as the sun burned down, but it hadn't cooled the air or cleansed it. The air still stank, a choking, feral, rotting stench as though the hospitals were pouring blood and bloody by-products into the sewers to create an urban slurry pit of human waste.

The vista Nova surveyed on the street could have been from any number of markets she'd visited while on business trips with her husband — Madrid, Buenos Aires, Paris — and it didn't fit into the carefully contrived Fodor concept of

Toronto, of Canada, thoroughly studied before her arrival. It was neither clean, world-class metropolis nor pristine and rugged wilderness, though it mightn't have surprised her to see a birchbark canoe rolling down the middle of the street.

Mrs. Philippa Maria Donahue's reality had shifted further as she slept, split itself off to play hide-and-seek behind some other lobe of her brain, so rather than succumbing to disorientation or doubt, which would have been logical reactions, her fantasy of a new life prevailed, caused her to float, content in a half-stupor, into her new neighbourhood. Her mood was vacationy, enhanced to a perfect pitch of otherness by the tropical heat and the feeling that she was working as an extra on a madcap television series. CUT TO: parenthetically shaped Chinese elders stocking rickety stalls with dangerous weights of produce. A catastrophic collapse, a regular primavera sidewalk. Perky young woman chases rolling tubers and presents them, laughing, to a tired-but-smiling immigrant.

Nova glanced at the bushel baskets and cardboard boxes set upon stolen milk crates; looked for novelty among creamy new, red, and sweet potatoes, Yukon Golds, dirty old dull-brown bakers. She saw unknown bok choy and Jerusalem artichokes, identified, to her frustration, by price but not name. The shop on the corner had its fruits and vegetables arranged as if by a food stylist for maximum use of colour. Lutein mangos and nectarines with patches of bright red like blood spots, oddly shaped but beautifully ripened field tomatoes, and a dozen varieties of greens were shaded, garnished themselves for a change, by flimsy umbrellas. Flats of perfect plump strawberries lined the back wall inside, too ripe to take any more sun before becoming freezer jam, and mushrooms the size of Nova's hand evoked the descriptive magic. She missed the stores with the stinky fruit and sugar cane, but did stop to sniff a variety of incense sticks on display.

Many shops tuned their stereos to the same station, so a Barry White song from her youth trailed her a few blocks, put a little funky glide in her stride, added a theme song to the morning.

Nova Philip promenaded in her fugue state along the main streets and consumed the sights and smells for breakfast. She thought of an old John Denver song about filling up senses and wondered how long that could sustain her. Since she couldn't pull more than the one line of chorus from her memory, she abandoned the idea, focused on observation while eating a peach.

Here was a derelict rowboat on a roof, converted to a planter above a fish shop. There, plastic cod heads with fierce looks seemed to poke through an awning to stare at their salted and splayed-out bodies stacked beside them. A couple of calamine mannequins, naked on a peaked dormer, looked alive, like they somehow enjoyed straddling burning shingles. Near the top of Augusta Avenue she went into Freshly Baked Goods for a croissant, but the place sold handknit sweaters, not cakes and cookies. A Million Articles did describe its dusty boxes of buttons and threads, and the Kensington Trading Post proved to be an excellent source of outdated appliances and electronics. Nova would have walked right by the Yes, Yes Store had a tape deck not been set out front among the hankies and hosiery. Marching music and a recorded voice chanting "Only twenty-five cents; nothing over fifty cents" lured her under a weary awning into a little cubbyhole of an establishment. The originator of the voice sat inside, wheelchair bound and bereft of huckster spirit. His merchant ventriloquism, spanning both space and time, caused church giggles to wrack Nova's shoulders, and she quickly left. She was able to laugh out loud in front of Courage My Love, and bought herself an amulet of bravery, a brightly braided bracelet she swore she'd never remove.

Sensory overload made her forget to worry about the steps she had taken, made her forget herself. She had always tried to see with wide eyes, but it was still only what she wanted to see, what had been suggested by the guidebooks, or a particular and personal agenda for being in situ. Confronted at each step with signs announcing Dementia; Exile; Noise, even her room above Asylum failed to shout its significance in an audible pitch. Courage My Love was what she needed most and so Courage My Love was what she saw.

She did recognize there was something unique about Kensington Market, some carefully crafted psychic wall or sensory illusion, fabricated over the past century as a magician's sleight of hand: the audience is kept focused on the surface while the woman in the box rolls out the false side to safety. She'd read in her guidebook that the Jews created the Market in the early years of the twentieth century, shut out of the Anglo business community, even here. They traded with each other from their doorsteps and from pushcarts, and somehow that original tradition still survived.

Kensington Market evolved as a clearing house for all manner of refugees. After the Second World War, the Portuguese settled in along with Ukrainians and Hungarians. The seventies saw Chinatown expand, and then the Vietnamese came. Hippies with persistent resolve followed, driven out of their Yorkville apartments, and were soon joined by musicians, painters, poets, and other free-spirited types seeking camouflage from the eighties world. Jamaicans and Latin Americans arrived and discovered cheap rents for establishing businesses, built once-crazy dreams of autonomy and self-sufficiency.

What her information failed to tell her, what Nova did not yet see, was that the community allowed to exist inside its ten-block box has no significance to an audience that secretly hopes for a bloody and gruesome mistake with one of the magician's blades.

And so, packs of nouveau-hippie chicks ride the subway in from the suburbs with Mom and Dad's credit card safely zippered in knapsacks, and for them the store names mean the best selection of flares or cords, multicoloured beads, airline flight totes to use as purses, compliments at school on Monday morning for finding a perfect pair of vintage Adidas. They don't bother to venture off Kensington Avenue, so they ignore the food, the privilege of abundance, never stop to think that the food nourished the formation of the Market, the way it does all life. Tradition and history and community are irrelevant to these searchers of fun wear. Their parents see a vast selection of cheeses, bread, and cheaper produce but less convenience than a supermarket, terrible parking, crawling traffic. They see dirt and E. coli, Poor-Peopleville, and wish for just a little more regard for their needs please. Kensington Market provides them with once-a-year entertainment shopping, an outing to the foreign-smelling premises of El Buen Precio, Akram's, Segovia, Sam Li. These may be the authentic stores of variety, putting the others to shame for their pretense, but they are out of place, replaceable.

In the spirit of a picnicky treasure hunt, Nova Philip poked around each of the stores that Saturday morning with the intention of determining their contribution to the quality of the Market. She isolated the exotic items particular to each: banana leaves and country-specific styles of chorizo, spicy beef patties, houses of spice or eggs or nuts, herbal remedies and good-luck air freshener.

Her Kensington Market had been ordered in an efficient separation of products, and she labelled the main roads, for simplified reference, as Fish Street, Clothes and Vegetable Avenues. How much easier life could be if all streets had such utilitarian names; a person would always know precisely what to expect from an address. Bay could become Money; University, more accurately, Hospital; and Yonge might easily be Long Street, since Sleaze could really apply only to a portion.

Three hours later, watching the passing lives from a stool at the corner of Fish and Vegetable, Nova drank two cups of black coffee. Her remaining objectivity was as precarious as a snowflake in the heat. If a landscape forms its people, seeps into their souls to define them, it was not the fault of Mrs. Philippa Maria Donahue that she had been cut off from her senses and was now overwhelmed to the point of irrationality. She had bought into the belief that a successful life was measured by the degree of sterility achieved. The world she methodically sought out effectively shut out the sensory as too frequently offensive. Fighting neighbours, barking dogs, and amplified music were other people's aural problems. The smells of exhaust or close foreign body odours were locked out whenever possible in hermetic vehicles scented with dangling pine trees. Unsightly images could be ignored or turned off with the press of a button. Taste alone was controllable, though tenuously, dependent upon the skill of the chef, and even that sense had mutated to mean something entirely different.

But now she thought she could effectively hide, here among the smells and noises and lives lived, escape the layers of lies that had threatened to suffocate her.

◆

Promptly at noon, an invigorated Nova Philip slipped off her stool and walked down Vegetable Avenue to find the Plate, though it was no longer really called that. The regulars used the reference to quickly determine longevity of association and its accompanying status of acceptance: the ten-year rule, an essential law of those with cause to distrust. An unseemly assemblage crowded the patio, but she spied Tommy sitting in the sun, attempting the weekend crossword with occasional input from a round table of less-than-shining knights.

"Hi," she said timorously from behind a low wrought-iron fence.

"Hey!" he shouted. "You found it! Welcome to the hottest patio in town. This, baby, is where the true 'in-crowd' hangs. In-ebriated, in-sensitive, in denial, but always in-teresting."

"Inept" would have best described Nova, but her fortifying thought was "insouciant," when she was told to grab a chair and join the crowd. All the seats were occupied, not only at his table, and she waited for a gentlemanly offer.

"Don't just stand there, girl. Git!"

Tommy pointed to a tall stack of extras at the far end of the patio. As Nova reached up to pull the top one down, an unpalatable soup of leaves and rainwater and pigeon shit splashed on her slip and on her painted toes. This was not what Nova Philip desired from a drinking establishment, and more, Tommy Gunn was consumed by his crossword, so introductions were not made. She stood there, insouciance quickly overshadowed by inarticulacy, and waited for a waitress to appear with a rag. One of the men at the table had a list of rehab clinics crudely printed on his sleeve, a sort of tour jacket of addiction. He rose to greet her, extending five aubergine fingers of a meaty hand.

"Richard. And yes, I've been to all these places, and no, none of them gave me the spiritual ecstasy necessary to replace my heaven of choice. Met some interesting people at the Betty Ford, though."

"My name's Nova."

"Enchanté, Nova."

Tommy looked up at Richard, said, "Seven letters for 'greeting'? FUCK OFF."

"If you're not going to pay attention to your guest, Gunn, someone else will."

"I'll pay attention to your pockmarked face, mate. A little rearranging would do it some good."

The waitress was occupied on the other side of the patio, at the entranceway, blocking the path of a stumbling old man. Nova kept sticking an arm up, half up, to try to get some service and the use of a rag, but the girl kept her back turned, kept shouting "Go to the park!" while she pointed across the road. "Go. To. The. Park."

Tommy looked up from his puzzle and observed the drama with only marginal interest.

"What do you suppose separates us from him?"

Nova turned around, shrugged.

"The fence."

She knew he was being metaphorical about the fineness of lines, knew it didn't apply to her, but wondered about the relevance to the rest of them.

"Surely it's more than that," she suggested, hoping for

confirmation that her companions for the afternoon were not so tenuously removed from Bowery bums.

"Okay. And three bucks for a pint. Speaking of which, you want to buy me one?"

Mrs. Philippa Maria Donahue had drinks bought for her, not the other way around. Nova Philip would have to accept such alterations to the fabric of that life, fit them in, and try to discover the benefits.

"If you pay a little attention to me like your friend here suggested," she responded. "Help me get this chair cleaned off for starters."

The men at the table exchanged glances, wonder, and a wee bit of envy. Tommy flashed gritted teeth in a false grin and told them, "Either ya got it, boys, or ya ain't."

"What are you going to do when your charm wears off, Tommy? When you're sitting around with your shirt undone and your huge hairy belly hanging out like Old Smokey over there?"

"I'll kill myself before that happens," he said, glancing at the man already snoring in the corner. "I mean, really."

He used a wad of napkins to remove the worst of the filth from the chair, and upon completion held it out for her with deliberate gallantry, said, "If I had a jacket, love, I'd throw it down for ye."

"I appreciate the thoughtfulness," said Nova, with sarcasm edging her words.

For a brief moment Tommy studied her, then reached out and pulled the black velvet scrunchee from her hair, releasing a wild cascade of curls down her back.

"Wow. Would you look at that, boys. Dig the porn-star hair."

The table concurred with Tommy's assessment, and Nova snatched the covered piece of elastic from his hand and pulled her hair back again in a little huff.

"Let your hair down, baby," said Tommy.

"It's too hot," she said, looking away.

"I'll say," he whispered in her ear.

She felt nauseous again, at the lower end of her belly, and frowned unknowingly.

"Don't get your knickers in a twist. You wanted attention, didn't say I had to be nice to you."

She wanted him to be nice. Needed it. Her day was going all pear-shaped from where it began.

"I'm not wearing knickers," she tried, paused for the effect, and added, "Where I come from, we call them panties."

"Where did you come from anyway?" asked Tommy. "The zone of zero funkativity?"

"I'm funky!"

"You ain't got the funk. I got the funk. That beav over there, she's got it."

"You don't think my dress is funky?"

"Clothes don't make you funky. Clothes is disco. Funk is inside busting out. Your hair, now that's funky. But you! You're way too uptight to be funky."

"No I'm not."

"No I'm not," he mimicked, piercing the air with unattractive notes. "Hmmm. Let's see. The funkativity quotient. One. Have you ever danced somewhere other than a club?"

"Such as?"

"The street, a table, in your living room maybe?"

He grabbed her hand before she had a chance to answer and pulled her to her feet. Tommy danced at her, limbs and pelvis composed of gel, a human lava lamp, while she held her ground.

"I'm shy," she said, pulling away.

"Of what?"

"People will think I'm nuts, or a tart."

"Here? If you can't funk here, you can't funk anywhere."

"I've got to go to the bathroom," she said, to escape. "Where's the ladies' room?"

"Ain't no ladies' room here," Tommy told her. "But there's a toilet with a chick on the door in the basement." Everyone laughed except Nova, and someone yelled out after her, "Make sure you lock it," and she did.

In the musty basement toilet, Nova shook out her hair and examined herself in a cracked mirror. She didn't think she could ever look like a porn star, even if she wanted to, which she did not. She did want to appear funky, but staring at her reflection, she most accurately appeared bland, unable to light the spark of charisma and energy that makes the plainest face glow. She wondered if it was the contrast, like the difference between male and female birds. He was without question a peacock, or a blue jay with that mean streak, and she was the female with less vibrant colour.

Yesterday, she had blamed it on being a wife, but she knew it was bigger than that, had suspected it was bigger than that for some time now. She felt like a building carefully and attractively designed to fit into a neighbourhood, one you might walk by every day for two years, never stopping to wonder what its purpose might be, until one day you finally take note and discover it is an electrical substation masquerading as a community centre or school.

As she stared, she had an awareness of being nothing, a

phony, considered it was partly Brendan's fault, but had to admit that she'd converted to the religion of staid before she met him, gradually stripped herself of the colour and charm that she knew she'd once possessed.

"Get a grip, Phillie. You can soak up a new personality around here, put one on some other way if the clothes aren't enough. Maybe there's one of those spray cans for the purpose."

She went upstairs with her hair undone.

"So what kind of music do you listen to, porn-star girl?" asked Tommy.

"I don't know. Alternative, I suppose."

"Alternative to what?"

"You know, not Top 40 or anything. Oasis, Radiohead, occasionally your Terminally Hip."

"That's a good one," laughed Tommy. "It's Tragically Hip, porn-star girl."

"Will you please stop referring to me as a porn-star girl. I find it quite offensive."

"Sorry, thought you might like a little self-image adjustment to go with the running away from home and new name."

Mrs. Philippa Maria Donahue obviously wasn't the first woman to run into the arms of Kensington Market, because the others at the table showed no surprise when this was said. She was not pleased that even this act was unoriginal, transparent, and now offered up for ridicule. She didn't understand where the animosity towards her was coming from, and the euphoria of her morning receded.

"I am adjusting," she replied. "In fact, I've spent the morning seeing."

"Seeing what?"

"Seeing. Like you told me."

He looked at her as though he didn't remember telling her anything. He looked at her as though she was a freak, even though Nova suspected he was the true odd man out.

"And what did you see?"

"Why they talk about Canada as being a cultural mosaic."

Tommy howled, not a howl of laughter, a great, insulting, demeaning noise. A howl of absolute derision.

"What's wrong with that?"

"Shall we issue you a stamp for your great discovery?"

"Why are you acting like such an arse?"

"Take another look, sweetheart. You're still so on the surface. Gotta see deeper than that. Stop being an achromat."

Her remaining buoyancy was now totally deflated, and Nova tried to fill herself back up with a pint of draught and half a package of cigarettes. She smoked mostly to provide a diversion, something to do so she wouldn't be perceived to be as lost and lonely as she felt. It was the best thing about smoking, something the purists didn't understand. A person could sit doing nothing, seem purposefully engaged in an activity other than being dismissed. She was often disgusted with herself when she smoked too much, swore to give it up, but whenever she found herself in these situations, cigarettes were like trusted companions.

Soon she had drunk enough draught to be a little belligerent herself and she asked Tommy what he meant by achromat.

"Colourless."

"What, you learn the big words in your crossword dictionary?"

The men at the table liked that, and Nova was grateful for a small show of friendliness through their laughter, even if it caused Tommy to snarl at her. Nova Philip accepted that a little such negativity was better than flatlining through life.

Tommy's attention was diverted by a woman across the street, waving at him from the doorway of the Kensington Pet Talent Agency.

"Shit, gotta go. Come watch the show." He finished his pint and was off, leapt over the railing with a quick look back to flaunt his act of disobedience, punishable by an embarrassing reprimand from a beleaguered boss who couldn't understand why his customers weren't content to behave in his establishment and simply use the gate.

The Pet Talent Agency was really a ruse for luring egocentric dog and cat owners onto its premises for grooming, one more example of someone cashing in on the city's obsession with making movies. Hollywood North needed prop pets, and the KPTA promised portfolios, custom grooming for bit parts, basic training in what the owners might expect from a surly casting agent feeling somewhat put out by having to find the right domestic animal with personality. These people transferred their own hopes and desires onto their pets the way a certain breed of parent will do with their children. Animal lovers, they blinded themselves to the actual cruelty involved in hot lights and repetitive work in the belief that their pets were the next Diefenbaker or Littlest Hobo or Rin Tin Tin. Autographed photos covered the walls, a stuffed Bullet replica sat in a corner, Santa's Little Helper and Ren were represented on tee-shirts for sale.

Tommy Gunn was called upon for the really difficult jobs, the ones requiring a fearless hand with the electric shears or the creation of a specific look. He could turn a scruffy dog into a purebred, or transform a good-natured Alsatian into a fierce guard dog with the application of a little red lipstick smeared around its muzzle.

The owner of one Snowball, a punkette poodle on the brink of losing her edge to age, requested a dramatic new look to distinguish her from the run-of-the-mill teacups that seemed to have taken over the Market. It was difficult to trust their presence, incongruous outside apartment towers with good addresses. The trend, spurred by a photo of some rock star looking hip and sensitive with a highly groomed Standard beside him, was for dog as fashion accessory.

Snowball, in fact, was a dirty urban mess. Slushpile, Slushy, even Slut would have been a more appropriate name. All six inches of her loved nothing better than a day of diving into garbage piles and picking absurdist fights with pit bulls and shepherds. She could get away with it too, particularly when in heat.

Tommy's task was to help her look mean and cool and fit to be owned by a 200-pound biker. He was taking her to an audition for a cellphone commercial and hoped that together they would become recognizable celebrities.

He set up a mini-stage in the window, as this was no ordinary gig. This was performance art. Tommy Gunn changed into a costume, transformed himself into Warren Beatty circa *Shampoo*, while the owner of the store put on a carny voice to solicit attention and encourage donations from passers-by.

Tommy bathed the wiry little beast in a bleaching solution to remove the stains and yellow that had crept into her coat. He set her on a table and slipped her tiny head through a noose clamped on its edge. Snowball struggled and slid off the table, dangled like a piñata for a moment, and when Tommy set her back on top, she bit him.

"You little bitch," he yelled, then realized her owner was watching. "That's what they are, buddy, I didn't mean anything." He suggested the large man go across the street for a beer while he did his thing, and stroked and cooed to demonstrate he really loved small overbred animals. As soon as the biker left, he gave a comic demonstration of how he was able to freeze this Snowball in a spastic expression with a pinch on the top of her neck. He applied green on her head and tail, fuchsia on her legs, and a bluish rinse on her torso. With the shaver in a surprisingly steady hand, he took her midsection down to bare skin. Her legs became sticks with chemical-pink cotton-candy balls around the feet. The green hair on her head was teased and backcombed and made all out of proportion with her thin neck. He added a rhinestone collar that hung like a bangle on an anorexic wrist.

When she was released from the noose, Snowball ran around the store in a frenzied state of dog beauty. Her owner cried when he saw her, out of joy rather than despair, and Tommy made ten bucks in the collection bin outside.

"Where'd you learn to do that?" Nova asked him.

"Nowhere, really. Lindy here needed some help one day, so I obliged. Most of the time it's straight grooming, but occasionally she gets a request like this one and asks me to do it. She's a bit conservative. Kinda like you. Now, I gotta run. See ya 'round, and if I don't see ya 'round, I'll see ya square."

Nova felt abandoned on the street, had thought she'd be entertained the entire day. A suspicion arose that she had been tricked into coming only to buy the drinks, and her conviction wavered.

May 14

They say a hole in the ozone layer is responsible. I blame my husband for this little death, and a new resentment threatens to send me off, not physically, but psychically, emotionally. My first act as a Canadian Resident is to methodically remove burnt particles from our little patio garden. In what feels like a slow motion replay of someone else's life, I cut the plants back in the event they aren't completely dead deep down in the roots, soak them, and wonder if the rain ever slants onto this patch of concrete or not. Affection, respect, even graciousness lie in a burial site under the loam of recent experience. With effort, I work shreds of these feelings to the surface and credit him with too much worry focused on our new life here to waste on a few herb pots.

A need for some sign of life propels me through the door unwashed, and I drag my disoriented self to a store at

Davenport Road where I am surrounded by decisions that are too difficult to make, so I ask the smiling Korean woman to make them for me and she is willing.

A good hour filled with that chore, another fifteen minutes chatting about gardening with the pleasant doorman whose job it is to assist laden-down residents. Now, the placement of my purchases requires careful consideration of colour and growth potential, a study of white plastic picks for sun and water requirements. Gentle removal from green plastic squares, a little root massage and separation. The earth is miraculously cool and calming in my palm. Daisies and geraniums, rosemary, basil, and oregano mix with the charred remains. I should remove them, the hopeless ones, but can't bring myself to pull them up.

What a minimal presence I've created, pathetic really, so inadequate. I stare at my choices in the planters, and the realization that two hours of labour have amounted to such a sorry garden tires me completely. Rather than continue my morning out of doors, I move inside to distance myself from the depressing effort and the mess of earth and discarded pots I don't have the energy to clean up. I imagine the patio might clean itself if a breeze ever decides to visit this part of the world.

Going from room to room, looking for distraction, all I notice is the peachiness of the place: the walls, the framed reproductions, threads of it in the upholstery. I'd thought it was ideal when we chose the condo two months ago, but now it seems so deliberately inoffensive, it offends. I can't imagine a life unfolding here, anyone's, and wonder if the decor was chosen for that effect, so the temporary residents won't experience unease about living with the things of someone else. There's nothing to hint at who was previously making love in the bed we're now sleeping in, and certainly nothing to inspire me in that direction.

I try to envision how I would decorate if it were really my home, where I'd place all the carefully selected antiques now sitting in a storage locker. There is nothing to be done, no escaping the droning colour, chosen, it seems, to accent the white noise of the air-conditioning. It's not just my preference for mouldings and hardwood floors, shady backyards, and front porches. There is no apparent way to install a bit of myself, and even if I enjoyed clutter, no place for it to accumulate, as every flat surface already has a purpose.

On the coffee table is a biography I began on the plane and abandoned when it failed to immediately draw me in. The face on the back is a sculpture of actual experiences, its lines and eyes and imperfections making it a perfectly interesting whole. Famous people must have odd lives — the really intelligent ones — must have difficulty separating the real, or living it, when constantly being watched. But it must be . . .

The telephone rankles me out of the reverie.

"Hello?"

"I'm so glad it's you, love. We've been worried sick since you left. How are you settling in?"

"I'm fine, Ma. Peachy, in fact, but a wee bit embarrassed about my behaviour."

"Ach, sure. Don't you mind about tha'. Have the two of you made up then?"

"I'm here, aren't I?"

"Tha' was not my question, girl."

No-good, incomprehensible tears come from nowhere, so I stare at the ceiling's white banality to force them to drip back inside. At least it isn't peach. That would send me over the edge.

"Phillie?"

"Yeah," I say briskly, and pause to swallow to steady the tremor in my voice. "I'll try to sort things with Brendan. I don't quite understand my reaction to all this. It makes no sense, but he . . ." I think carefully for the right word, the exact one that could clarify it for us both. "He suddenly repulses me."

Ma pauses. "That's a bit harsh."

"I know, I know. But it's the truth. I nearly cried when I saw him at the airport, actually thought of walking back through the gate and coming home."

"Ah, Phillie. It's never easy leaving home and there's no denying you've been through a rough patch. Losing a baby can be difficult on a marriage, but he's not a bad man, is he? He hasn't been treating you poorly."

"No, he's not a bad man," I say.

"Try to make the most of it then, love. I know Brendan hasn't really been there for you during this, has spent too much time away from home."

"I thought absence was meant to be a positive thing, the heart fonder and all that."

Ma laughs the laugh she uses when about to impart great wisdom.

"Cold is the pie out of the oven too long," she says.

"I'm not a pie, Ma," I reply, smiling for the first time in weeks, months maybe.

"You know what I mean, Philippa. You need to warm things up again."

"I know, I know, and I'll try. Listen, I'll write you a long letter once I'm myself again. Okay?"

"That's fine. You know we're here. There's always a bed for you."

"I know. Take care."

The condo walls close in when I sever communication, isolate me, shrink me to an insignificant speck. The atmosphere is alienating, makes me feel out of place, makes me think I will drown in the empty peach time around me. How does a person swim through the thickness of such sensory emptiness?

"Fake it 'til you make it." Another of Ma's pearls.

In the bedroom that is meant to be ours, but is more correctly "the," I rummage through my suitcases for something to wear with the power to instill good humour, but my clothing is all about designer and logo, not "I feel good today," or even "look at me." A navy sleeveless shift of semi-sheer material looks as though it might accomplish both, definitely the latter, if I accessorize with tiny white panties.

I grab what remains of the money left by Brendan, grudgingly, it seemed, didn't it, and embrace the din and solid heat on Avenue Road. I alter my walk from its earlier plod to that of a capricious young woman, tilt my head back in defiance of visible underwear.

Yorkville, the rental agent told us, was once the hippie headquarters of Toronto, but not a hair of anti-establishment remains: no record shop, no musical blitz on the tastefully umbrella'd patios, each occupied by a mass of identical people. I have no cause to enter the stores, no need for a thousand-dollar scarf or silken gown. I wish they were stores of necessity, so I could chat someone up for a few minutes, share a complaint about the humidity being worse than the heat.

Finally, a shop able to lure this distressed spirit inside. Lovecraft, it's called, and I spend a pleasant half-hour giggling at the rubber devices of desire, their creative names in particular. We women have a marvellous choice of Pocket Rocket, Clitterific, Dolphin, the last shaped as such in the event the realistic versions are too . . . what? Male? Too lifelike and depressing when lacking the real thing? Maybe male partners find them threatening. I debate purchasing a sleek black dildo and asking Brendan to play with it, but then I spy the corncob, and it frightens me out of the place.

One of those supermarket bookstores on the next street promises a more appropriate distraction. The air inside is cool and fragrant, a pleasing combination of coffee and printers' ink. Soft jazz music plays throughout, but is punctuated by a barrage of frenzied paged announcements that almost sound like poetry in my confused state. The fiction department is craftily situated on the third floor, in the back reaches of the store, to oblige customers to trek by tables of suggested reading choices.

I'm looking for escape and total absorption, but I also think of the next time I'm stuck with Brendan's friends without the correct retinue of references and grab the first suggestion off the Canadiana table.

Back home, not home, housed, I settle into a corner of the overstuffed couch, "shabby chic," as it was described by the rental agent. It is the one thing I still like about the decor, despite its shade. I read and smoke for the rest of the afternoon, pause only to wonder at the timeliness of the gift, the reassurance in my hands that others could find enough inspiration in this country to write about it. By the time Brendan arrives from work, I'm halfway through the novel and have completely forgotten about preparing anything for dinner.

"Brendan, hello. I'm so sorry. I bought a new book this

afternoon and lost myself completely. Could we go out for dinner?"

His irritation stretches across his face in well-defined lines, causes me to think of Ma's warnings about making faces and how they will stay like that. I can see they do, in a way, if a single expression is favoured throughout a life.

"Sure. What do you feel like?"

"Oh, I don't know. Is it still revolting out there?"

"It's cooling down a little."

"Why don't we go somewhere in Yorkville with a patio, watch the world go by, and all that?"

"Fine. I'll just put on a clean shirt."

"Would you like a drink?"

"Please."

I read to the end of the page and reluctantly lay down the bookmark. The breakfast counter between the living room and kitchen is set up as a bar, well stocked with good scotch, Russian vodka, cognac. Is it relief I feel that Brendan was not so devastated by our loss as to prevent him from maintaining these little comforts, or am I simply pleased to see we have gin? Both. If he can get on with the little things in life, he might not question and pressure me about the big ones. I mix drinks in tall glasses, remember to rim the edges with lime, the way he taught me, and as an afterthought make mine a double.

"Slainte," I say, handing him a deliberately weak cocktail.

"Cheers."

When I move out from behind the counter, the late-afternoon sun shines through the glass patio doors, and through my dress, apparently, because Brendan nearly chokes.

"Jesus, Phillie, did you actually go out dressed like that?"

"Like what?" I ask, looking down at myself.

"You can see your underwear right through that dress."

"Oh, Brendan." I feel so weary and tense, and take a large sip of my drink. "Of course not. I took my slip off because it was too hot. I'm so glad you noticed, else I might have forgotten. Imagine the looks we'd get strolling along to dinner!" I laugh because I'd managed to keep sarcasm out of my voice. "People would assume you were a visiting businessman with a mistress or escort or something tawdry. How awful!"

"Are you slagging me?" He adds more gin to his glass, proving his predictability.

"Slagging you? Not at all." I kiss his cheek to reassure him and go to find a half-slip.

"Be a good girl," I tell my reflection and try to purge my system of the urge to act out by sticking out my tongue. It remains, though, like a five-foot tapeworm slowly unwinding in my bowels and inching its way up my throat. No. That's a tickle worm, just as long; the tape ones go out the other end.

The air outside is oppressive still, and the nylon slip traps moisture like cling wrap. I hate how legs sweat, calves in particular, didn't even know they could before coming to this putrid, humid place. I mean, do they even have pores? I remember the first time we came to visit Brendan's family, years ago. It was an early heat wave like this, and his parents had no air-conditioning. I woke up in the middle of the night thinking that bugs were crawling over me, but it was only this. I curse Brendan's overdeveloped sense of decorum as the sweat trickles down my thighs. What's the point of a breezy dress if you block out the breeze? I cast a sideways glance at him to see if he shares my discomfort, and his condition irritates me further.

"What sort of deodorant are you using these days?"

He looks at me as though this is the most irrelevant question ever posed, but I've seen him spend a good ten minutes comparing scents and promises in the drugstore.

"I don't know. Why?"

"You're not sweating. I'm drenched."

"I do not wish to sweat, therefore, I'm not."

I turn my head to roll my eyes. Move my lips in a mimic of his self-aggrandizement.

Walking with him embarrasses me. He is so visibly anal that he might as well carry around a tube of hemorrhoid cream. I don't think he's ever walked somewhere just for the pure pleasure of it. His pace is too hurried for the heat, too purposeful to take in any scenery.

I want only to glide down the street, sashay, and swing. I want my man's hand to slide from my waist to feel my ass, to use the opportunity of walking together to enjoy it, own it. Soon it will drop and dimple. Soon I'll be viewed as mutton dressed as lamb if my skirt is too short or has a hand on it. It will be grotesque. Even I can reconcile that.

We round the block at Cumberland and are beckoned by a hostess to chill out on the rooftop patio at Hemingway's, a pubbish restaurant in a converted house.

"Will this suit you, love?" I ask, desperate to get off the street and away from the thoughts that keep streaming through my head.

"It's fine."

We climb the steep staircase to a tiered patio, filled to near capacity with thirsty after-workers. A table is available on the second level, next to a large party identifiable by their uniforms as booksellers from across the street, raucously trading stories of the day's unreasonable customers.

"What do you say I give Brook a ring? See if he and Ashley care to join us?"

Brook works with Brendan, and although the couple are not people I would choose as friends, I can't bear the thought of an entire evening alone with my husband.

"Sure. Brook's always good craic," I lie.

Brendan pulls out his cellphone and calls Brook's. Who is really so important as to require constant communicative accessibility? I doubt omnipotent men carry these pocket invasions of privacy. I feel self-conscious, guilty of pretension by association, and glance at the booksellers for a reaction. They are oblivious, of course, with their own world to consume them, even when Brendan stands and starts pacing as people with cellphones feel obliged to do.

"Brook. Philippa and I are having dinner and drinks at Hemingway's . . . Really? . . . Let me look . . ." Brendan walks to the railing and looks across a small laneway. He motions for me to do the same, and I reluctantly obey. Ashley waves like she's the Queen of England. Brook snaps his fingers at a waiter. "Cool. See you shortly."

"I didn't know people actually did that anymore," I say.

"Do what?"

"Snap fingers at waiters."

"That's just Brook being controversial. He doesn't mean anything by it."

"Does he whistle at them too?"

"Sometimes."

Brendan smirks at a particularly fond whistling memory. Breathe. Behave. Say something quick instead of picking a fight.

"What are the odds that they'd be right next door?"

"Brook isn't exactly the Queen Street type."

"What's the Queen Street type?" I ask.

"Black clothing. Piercings. Funny hair."

This last is accompanied by his famous one-eyebrow lift, the one that reaches to his scalp and creates a look far more ridiculous than the one it is intended to scorn. He's commenting on my own hair, a pulled up, butterfly-clipped bun which is cool, in the original way of that word, fun, but perhaps just a little muttony.

A waitress comes to take our order, and Brendan requests two more chairs.

"You'll have to look around for them yourself. I'm way busy."

"Great!"

"I'll go," I offer, rising to avoid a scene.

"No, no. They're my friends. I'll do it."

Brendan returns triumphant with chairs and our guests.

"Philippa! We've been wondering when we'd finally have the chance to get to know you better. Did you get everything packed up?" Brook kisses the air above my cheeks and leaves a stale, boozy scent — scotch, I think, since noon — clinging to the humidity around me. So that's the story. Brendan would never discuss anything remotely emotional, never admit to marital difficulties or complain about me. Someone might suspect his life is less than perfect. No, I've been toiling away in moving purgatory.

I can't bear to look at the big phony, say, "It wasn't much, really. I used the time to say a few farewells," chipper sounding, pleased to be here. "Hello Ashley. You're looking very fresh in this heat. I asked Brendan how he managed, but he apparently has some sort of willpower not familiar to me."

"Ice-water baths. Brings the blood temperature right down. Keeps the skin young and firm too."

"Lovely."

"It really is. You should try it. Throw some cucumber in, you'd think you were at a spa."

"I bet."

As usual, I'm expected to find common ground with the other woman at the table, and it requires more effort than I'm prepared for at the moment.

"Do you need a place to work out?" Ashley asks, then, without waiting for an answer, continues. "My club's the best, brand new and women only, which has its benefits, just up the street, and killer aerobics classes." Ashley is relentless, one of those narcissistic talkers requiring only a body — any body — at whom she can direct her voice. And she's a should-er to boot. Dieting musts follow her exercise tips and I absolutely have to shop at someplace or another. I barely need to nod or grunt encouragement, so it's quite easy to zone out this Chatty Cathy doll. I eavesdrop on our neighbours, listen to their full-bodied laughter, and strain to piece together their references to posts and isms. *They* are male and female talking together, talking about Ideas, not cucumber baths. It's not that I'd have anything to contribute to the discussion, but I wouldn't mind just listening and learning something for a change.

"What do you say, Phillie? You haven't seen enough of the city."

I'm being addressed by a male voice, Brendan's voice. "Sorry? I was distracted by that loud table over there."

"Brook has invited us to play pool, to 'shoot some stick,' as he calls it, down on College Street."

"What about dinner?"

"It's not your average pool hall. We'll grab something there."

"I don't know . . ."

"Come on, Phillie. We've been nowhere in the city. I read recently College Street is now considered one of the best neighbourhoods in North America, all renos and good restaurants, but I haven't been there in years."

"Okay, okay! As long as you're all patient with me."

"Don't worry, I can't play worth shit. Geometry and all that." Ashley waves the air, as though geometry is an irritating bug.

"We'll hop in a cab. Go to the Clearspot."

Ashley drones on about knowing the owners, not even attempting to sound like she's not bragging.

"They opened up just before the boom on the strip," she says. "Are at the edge of it, still hoping it'll creep east."

◆

Apparently, the boom has still not yet crept east, because the Clearspot is empty. Brook explains to me, in a somewhat patronizing voice, that the lack of customers is a result of Torontonians' obsessive relationship with their patios. Tables and chairs are always accessible on unseasonably warm days, and the best restaurants install outdoor heaters to facilitate a month-long extension of patio drinking at either end of the season. To go indoors on a hot summer night is to waste one of only twenty or so opportunities to enjoy a beer on a patio.

"Ask any Torontonian," he says. "They'll tell you how much better beer tastes out of doors."

"Really?" I reply, not exactly polite because I'd much prefer to test the beer theory myself than be stuck inside a dark basement bar. I should try to get along, but boredom with these people, with the whole stinking world really, weighs on me, causes the return of the urge to act out. I stay quiet and try to lose my unreasonable bad temper and anxiety through the music. Tom Waits's gravelly voice fills the converted warehouse space, seems to bounce off the rails of the tables as perfect bank shots into my ears.

"How brilliant to play his music in a pool hall," I think I say, but since no one responds, maybe not. I've noticed this strangeness all day, an inability to isolate my voice from my thoughts. I wonder if it's a type of Tourette's syndrome, if *they* actually hear the involuntary words coming out of their mouths.

"Shall we do the partner thing?" asks Brook. "Couples?"

"I'd prefer playing singles," I reply. "To give myself enough shots to warm up."

"Well, well, well," he says. "Perhaps you'd like to be first then?"

"I don't mind, really."

"Flip for break."

I remove my sandals to leverage my shots, make six in a row, ending with a near miss that places my final ball in fine shape for cleaning up.

"Patient while you smoke us?" Brook asks. "Is that what you meant back at Hemingway's?"

"It's a good table is all. That and the music. Music's always important."

"Where did you learn to play pool?" asks Brendan suspiciously.

"Josh, my best friend when I was a teenager, had a table in his rec room. When the rest of the world was dating, we hung out at his place, listened to depressing music, and convinced ourselves it would be more fun to be pool sharks than go on dates any day. I haven't played in ages, though it's amazing how it just comes back."

Brendan doesn't care for this aspect of his wife, I can tell by the firm set of his mouth, the dismissive quick up-and-down movement of his eyes. It's clear that not only does he think I appear cheap, he doesn't at all appreciate not knowing these things about me. As punishment for making him feel foolish, he orders another pint without offering one to me and keeps his distance from the table and game by talking too loudly to Ashley. I finish off matter-of-factly and shake Brook's hand firmly, the way I was taught to at such times, like a lad.

"You're up, Dan," he says. "Beer, Phil?"

"Phil! No one's called me Phil in ages. Thanks, Brook."

Brendan removes the balls from the pockets and methodically rolls them along the trendy purple felt.

"Shall we put some stakes on the table, darling?" I ask.

"Such as?"

"How about a back massage. Thirty minutes."

"Why not some real stakes? Twenty dollars, say?"

"I have no money with me."

"Oh. Okay then."

He knows that — the big jerk — is trying to show me who's still in charge.

"Rack 'em up then," I say, roll my head and sigh dramatically.

Brendan proves to be competent at the game, but I'm motivated, possibly at the testosterone stage of my cycle considering the aggression I feel. I haven't played in ten years, since I learned some guys don't like girls to be better than them at games, but I can see every shot as clearly as if there were charts drawn on the felt. The beer goes down well with the tension and perfectly sunk balls, the near misses that make you chalk your cue in response. For the rest of the evening, I enjoy watching my husband pout and sulk between bouts of concentrating pool-face. The more miserable he becomes, the gayer it makes me, until he can't stand it any longer and suggests we call it a night.

This novel supremacy over him is an aphrodisiac for me, and the double gin plus four pints of lager have loosened my limbs and my tongue. In the condo's mirrored elevator, I rub against his rigid body, slide my hands along his thighs.

"I'm feeling incredibly sexy."

"I can see that."

I take his hand and place it under my dress.

"But can you feel it?"

"Philippa!"

Not Philippa, Phil. I feel like a Phil right now.

"You know what I saw today? A beautiful vibrator. I almost bought it."

"What stopped you?"

"I wasn't certain you wouldn't take it wrong, as an insult or threat."

"Well, what is the point of something like that?"

"Just play."

I lower my body slowly and kiss his belly, stroke his hips, witness success.

Inside our unit, I lead Brendan to the couch and begin to undress him. My fingers move deftly through the buttons of his shirt and lightly brush his chest. I push him gently down on the couch and follow onto his lap. Because I don't want to look directly into his eyes, I concentrate on his neck, his ear, and he pulls me down to him, clamped against him. I release myself and stand, lift my dress slightly, and leisurely remove the hateful slip and little white panties while he watches. He quickly removes his trousers and boxer shorts and I lower myself onto him, slowly, teasing him a little before applying my full weight. He manoeuvres me onto my back, of course, and I slide us both towards the armrest for leverage.

"Fuck me." A whisper.

It interrupts his stroke.

"Don't stop. Come on. Fuck me."

He obeys, to my amazement, and shudders silently and as though against his will. He catches his breath and withdraws, puts on his pants, and goes for a drink.

"Where the hell did you learn that?"

"What?"

"To act like a whore."

"You didn't enjoy it?"

"That's not the point."

"I think it's exactly the point."

"You did this with someone else?"

"Of course not."

He turns and struts to the bedroom. Slams the door behind him.

The sensible course of action is to leave him alone until we are both sober in the morning, but I have that pent-up energy feeling that I really need to get out of my system before sleep will come. I only wanted to make him see the world doesn't have to be all dullness and the missionary position and one-sided satisfaction.

"Try to see it as a positive thing," I say from the doorway. "Don't all husbands wish their wives could be a little more like a mistress and less like a wife? Isn't that why they take mistresses in the first place?"

"I haven't taken a mistress."

"Yet. It would only be a matter of time."

"So you thought you'd beat me to it?"

"I never thought of it. It didn't happen."

"Somehow, I don't believe you, Philippa. Besides, you're too drunk."

"I'm not. Man oh man, I just wanted a little change."

"Right now, Philippa, you disgust me. If you won't be comfortable on the couch, I'll sleep there."

"No, no. I'm the baddy. It's my lot to suffer for it. May I take a blanket, or do you have a hair shirt I might slip on?"

The blanket comes at me through the darkness, hits me in the head.

"It's odd, Brendan. You didn't seem disgusted when your . . ."

"Get out."

◆

I hear him making coffee, and roll over to face the back of the couch so I won't have to worry about my eyes accidentally opening. He's angry still, and is trying to wake me up by letting cupboards slam. He won't get the satisfaction of it, though. We've been in this territory before, and I know what to expect from him: silence, avoidance, the grown-up version of punishment. Likely a three-day stint, at least. Maybe longer. He went two whole days without speaking to me when I complained about the orgasm thing. Mind you, I could have been more sensitive, but it had been so close, for so long, that I exploded at him and asked if there wasn't something he could do about being a two-stroke wonder. Not those words exactly, of course. In the end, I blamed PMS and faked it occasionally to make him feel better.

When he arrives home, it's only to change his shirt and

throw the silence at me before leaving again. If we are in each other's presence, I make deliberate discord to win a round. On Monday, I prepare dinner as an offering. We sit in our auditory blackout and my knife scratches across the plate. A fork disengages from my grip with a clatter. Brendan pretends he doesn't hear. If I speak, he listens politely.

"North American silence torture," I've labelled it, and for relief during his absence, a cacophony fills the space. I talk to myself, to the plants, to imaginary people who are not quite friends — that would be nutty. I tune in the CBC on the radio and talk back to the hosts. Music arouses the emotions I'm expected to suppress, and I dance them out, sing them out, or sit to feel the notes stirring the base of my neck.

The vacuum cleaner has become an ally, along with every other appliance that whirrs, drones, hums, or rumbles. They are allies in my solitude and when my husband brings his juvenile muteness home. In this way, I stay sane and ultimately win the petty game. Satisfaction, however, is elusive.

He breaks the silence on Friday afternoon, day seven, with an invitation from Brook. Selfish bastard, only thinking of getting away and didn't have the balls to say we're not getting on.

"Just what we need," I say. "Brilliant," I add, in case I sounded sarcastic. Mary, Mother of God. Help me. A whole weekend of charades.

When I step out of the car, I almost understand the four-hour traffic nightmare required to get us here. Almost, not entirely. There is some other aspect to it that I don't quite get, a sense of drama and false camaraderie usually reserved for small collective disasters or accidents, snowstorms and fire drills and the like. Halfway through the journey, we stopped at a road-side stand, a place reportedly so popular the government built a second parking lot and walkway across the highway to avoid further traffic jams. After idling irritably in traffic for two hours, we then stood patiently in a snaking half-hour lineup for burgers and fries, and those who travel the same route on a regular basis spoke amicably of the shared experience with strangers: "All the way from Barrie," etcetera, etcetera. "Aren't we the good little troupers," they seemed to say.

But the air at the cottage definitely ministers an aro-matherapy the naturopaths try to simulate and bottle. Smelling it here, I know the mood they try to replicate is this, though the nuances of pleasant memories it is meant to summon forth are yet to be revealed.

Through a wall of glass is a large view of a tiny lake, ringed with cottages on expansively private lots, each with a dock and a flagpole. Brook takes us outside and boasts that the wraparound deck allows access to the sun all day. It is just setting behind a fringe of trees, and we settle into deep Adirondack chairs with icy cold beers. A period of silence allows me to take a few deep breaths and listen to a soothing whisper of leaves in the evening breeze.

"Why so many flags?" I ask Brook.

"I think it goes back to the days when Americans owned a lot of the property up here. The tradition lingers."

"Americans are more partial to flags than Canadians?"

Brendan chortles unattractively through his nose.

"I think it's a charming and refreshing question," Brook tells him, tells me: "Most of the so-called Canadian identity is based on being less American, and that includes flag-waving."

"I see," I say, though I don't. I see very little difference. In fact, most Canadians I've met are trying desperately to be as American as they possibly can be. An instinct tells me it is the wrong view to hold.

"Did you summer here as a boy?" asks Brendan.

When did the seasons become verbs to him? Are they really so crucial to this country that they have been elevated from nouns, provided with double usage? What exactly does that imply, anyway? Entirely, I suppose, the entire season, exclusivity.

"My family has summered here for fifty years."

"Do you come up often now?" I ask. "Do you, um, weekend?" I don't know if this noun too has been transformed into a verb, but since no one comments, I suppose it has.

"I have to share it with my sister, Janice. She has a couple of rug rats, and it's just not the same when they're around. We try to divide it up, but every year it's the same and we always fight over holidays. I suggest she doesn't need the long weekends as much as I do — she doesn't work — but her husband is a real prick with an unreasonable sense of fairness."

"So buy them out," says Brendan, always in the role of black-and-white solution-provider, as though the vast amount grey in the world just doesn't exist, let alone colours.

"Her sentimentality is not for sale."

"I'm not certain I'd want to give it up either," I say, not trying to be antagonistic, but knowing it will seem that way. "And if you don't, why should your sister?"

"Because they can afford their own. Besides, it's always been passed down to the male in the family. My father died before he made the proper arrangements, so it's my mother's, really. Janice is a true suckhole and brings her up to visit with the grandchildren, has convinced her that it's all about family and memories, not real estate."

"We used to rent a cottage every summer," says Ashley. "Then one year, we stopped going. I thought we owned it, that it was my birthright to summer at a cottage. One of the biggest disappointments in my life was discovering it wasn't. Worse than the Santa Claus thing. Now, I get into a snit if I don't get up to one at least once a year. In fact, I used to be a complete cottage slut, spending the winter lining up invitations."

"I remember," replies Brook, sighing. "I used to get the best hummers around the May two-four weekend."

Ashley shrugs with faux coyness. "It's still worth your while."

I smirk at Brendan as he stares at Ashley's mouth, very nearly drooling. I want to point it out to the sanctimonious git, score a point to get even for the nose chortle.

"Do you guys want to do a line?" asks Brook.

"Sure," says Brendan, too quickly. I shoot him a quizzical look and he stares me down, quashes my objection with a look that says "I dare you to say a word," so I just watch as my husband becomes a more manic version of his uptight self — quite fascinating, really, because I didn't know it was possible. When Brook suggests water-skiing with a flashlight when his friends with the speedboat arrive, Brendan thinks it's some kind of bright idea, and this I cannot let pass.

"Do you think you're living in a beer commercial or something?" I ask.

"Wives don't nag in beer commercials."

"Coke certainly agrees with your present state of mind. Perhaps I should join you and we could just duke it out."

"Come on, Philippa. What's gotten into you?" asks Brook.

"Ask him. I'm going for a swim."

"I'll go with her," says Ashley. "I think we need a cleansing dip to eliminate the stress of the city. Perhaps you boys could build a fire for our return."

The sun is fully down by now, so we use the water-skiing flashlight to navigate the long meandering pathway to the lake. Once on the dock, I turn my face to the sky and the stars. "Look at that," I say to Ashley.

"What?"

"The sky."

"So?"

"It's the most incredible sky I've ever seen. The moon, so many stars. I never knew there were so many stars, that the moon could be that bright."

"It's just the sky." Ashley pulls off her clothes, dives in the water, and comes up with a scream like she's just been laid. "Now, this is gorgeous."

I'm torn between staying on the dock with the sky and joining a naked woman I hardly know in the water. "Is it cold?" I ask.

"Freezing, but you'll love it. Makes you feel refreshingly alive."

Mosquitoes settle the dilemma, and I strip and quickly enter the cold, muffling darkness, stay underwater until my lungs hurt and my limbs tingle, because it's a bit like hiding from the world. I paddle quickly towards the dock feeling closer to freezing to death than refreshingly alive, and a motorboat rumbles through the silence, the voices on board floating easily to the shore. A small lamp bounces across the water in our direction.

"Is that you, Sondra? Jemmy?" shouts Ashley.

"Ashley? Cut the motor, Anton."

"Hang on, we're getting out."

Ashley beats me to the dock, and as she pulls herself up the ladder she flexes gracefully like a gymnast on uneven bars. The boat's light flashes at her taut white buttocks, and the two women on board giggle.

"Stop it. You'll send the mozzies right there." Ashley doesn't rush for her towel, instead she allows Anton to get a good look at the body she works so hard to perfect. After all, he could be a cottage owner.

I, on the other hand, make sure my towel is well within reach before scrambling onto the dock, but the light flashes at me just as I bend to pick it up.

"That's what I like to see," shouts Anton. "Assume the position." They laugh, and I wonder if it's at me, wonder if I look inadequate to these people, if there are certain signs they look for and can use to identify their inferiors, like the Brits with speech, like if you don't know the seasons are verbs. They can do it with horses, can't they? Tell good breeding from teeth and mane and muscle systems?

We all trek up to the cottage and there are great loud hellos and the slapping of backs, so I slip off to the bedroom to avoid seeming sulky. I'm not, not really, but I don't think I'll enjoy those people, don't think I can bear to watch Brendan be happy among them. I certainly have no energy to fake it myself. I wish it were a quiet group, content to read by the fire and listen to the night. That seems like the correct activity for such a place. I can nearly hear the silence outside, but their voices leave the cottage and are funnelled by the deck around the little building, straight back in the open window. Wraparound deck, wraparound sound. Brendan comes in to get his swimming trunks and glances with a careful air of disinterest in my direction.

"I just wanted to be quiet."

"We're going water-skiing."

"It's really cold."

"We have wetsuits."

"Be careful."

He takes his suit with him rather than undress in front of me. I wait for their voices to get smaller, but they don't. Down on the dock, the men shout and the women screech. Someone gets pushed into the lake and the splash is followed by "fucking cunt." I shut the window and turn off the light.

The darkness heightens my sense of hearing and the distant laughter, the juvenile behaviour. The otherness of their idea of fun brings back memories of being shut out at boarding school. It was just like this, down to Ashley's naked prancing on the dock. Being a bit of a tomboy, I didn't have the proper training necessary to fit in there.

At fifteen, sent away to fix my rebellious spirit, to save me from damaging influences, I was different. It's wrong to be different at fifteen, not tolerated in girls' dormitories, the torture chamber for adolescents deemed too fat, too ugly, too unusual. Survival there was rooted in the principle of cloning.

I don't blame them for sending me away, really. Josh's parents caught us, half dressed, smoking pot in his basement. We didn't even like each other in that way, but were both feeling so lonely, with hormones we didn't know what to do with. The most humiliating memory I have is of his mother calling me a slut and marching me down the street to my house. Da told me he would have stayed in Belfast if he'd wanted me to wind up pregnant and with a waster for a husband. Ma went on and on about being disappointed, and I wished she'd just been angry.

The rites of passage at the school were established day one, lines drawn, rank carved in stone. The pretty girls strutted about naked while I wore an undershirt and pants at all times to hide the fact that I had no breasts to speak of. Once, I allowed Mary Flanigan to dress me up for a dance. I didn't know why she wanted to, she wasn't even a friend. She brought me one of her brassieres, a padded thing that I didn't nearly fill out, and she gave me tissues to stuff in it. We giggled a little, and I was so grateful for that toss of hope. But at the dance, a dreamy guy tried to feel one of them during a slow song, Elton John it was. I'll never forget it. I slapped his hand away and he told me Patty O'Reagan let him last time.

"Then go find her," I said, lessened by a boy for the first time, and he did. I had to endure them as they whispered and looked at me and laughed. Soon everyone seemed to be whispering and looking and laughing at me, and I guessed Mary had set the whole thing up for that purpose.

There was a really rich girl at school, can't remember her name, who had *Seventeen* magazine sent each month, then placed orders with her ma for Love's Baby Soft and Bonne Bell cosmetics, Jordache Jeans to tuck into Frye boots, leg warmers, and Tretorn runners. We all filled out the questionnaires in the common room to determine if boys liked us, learned the Scarsdale diet, and followed Jane Fonda's workout video. We learned to compare and compete, not for grades, not for athletics, but for bodies and boyfriends.

Those magazines were my hope. They offered the glossy key to conforming, and during the first summer break, I enlisted Ma's help with my transformation into a reasonable replica of a girl. Second year was easier as a result. I was allowed in on the fringe of the pretty crowd and let the boys touch my real breasts, though what thrill they got, I don't know. By third year, I was like a *Seventeen* model. I graduated to *Cosmo* at college, *Glamour*. The girls taught each other to puke, and I was suddenly envied for my lack of shape. It elevated me, and I flaunted it, never once looked back to see where the tomboy went, though a lingering distrust of other women remains with me.

Funny to remember those times now, how the angst can swell up and seem so close, only a little less significant. I still don't enjoy feeling like an outsider, even if I bring it on myself.

◆

Brendan chooses that night to finally spit out the question. Drunk, wet, rushing from the skiing or the coke, he shakes me awake, out of a dream about searching for the right shade of lipstick to wear to the prom.

"I need to know why you were so relieved. Was it not my child?"

"It's not about you. Not everything in the world is about Brendan Donahue. It's all about me."

"Of course it's about me."

"I'm half asleep, Brendan. Can we talk later?"

"No, we can't talk later. You're ruining the weekend for me, for everyone in fact."

"Me? I really don't think this is the time or place to discuss this, and I certainly don't think someone who's putting cocaine up his nose has any right to throw stones."

"I have a right to know the truth."

"Please keep your voice down." I take a deep breath and let it out in a statement sounding like a sigh. "I was scared."

"Of what?"

"Of the responsibility. Of the irreversibility."

"Couldn't you talk to me about it?"

"No. I didn't believe I could."

"Do you respect me?"

Not even love. Maybe he equates love with respect.

"It's not about respect, either. It's about life."

"That's a no, then?"

"I didn't say that."

"So there isn't someone else?"

"It's not always because of someone else, or sex, you know."

"So what is it then?"

"You really want to know? Fine. I'm afraid I will disappear."

"Have you thought about a psychiatrist?"

"No."

"Do you think you should?"

"I'd like to just try to find another way to make it all seem okay."

"Like how?"

"I don't know. Can you just give me some time? A month, say? Humour me for a bit, see what we can do?"

"Go see my doctor, at least. I'll make an appointment."

Brendan's solution to everything is taking control of the situation. I once liked that quality in him. Now it makes my shoulders tense, makes me want to grab the reins to my life back out of his hands, in whatever way necessary. I don't want his solutions. I'm now capable of finding my own, in my own time.

◆

A barking dog outside the open window wakes me, but Brendan doesn't stir, and when I leave the bedroom I can hear people are still asleep all around me. It's an unanticipated bonus for waking early, such quiet a luxury. The kitchen is filled with unfamiliarity, an old-fashioned percolator incomprehensible to me, but a large jar of stale instant crystals promises a caffeine jolt. It is a cottage apparently without a kettle, so I fill a saucepan with bottled water. How can a cottage not have a kettle when it has a microwave and dishwasher?

The muddy coffee tastes fine in the fresh air, goes down well in my reclined position on the dock. The cushion on the lounger is slightly damp from the dew and it emits a fragrance of sun cream, canvas, a bit musty. There are loons on the lake, the birds on the dollar coins they refer to as loonies. One of the birds trumpets sadly, and I wonder if it's because it has a coin named after it.

There's a backhoe rumbling down the lake somewhere, competing with a hammer to send the most irritating noise across the water. Thank God for the crickets, the chipmunks rattling the leaves loud as footsteps. The sun is trying to outsmart the clouds, to melt them away with help from a wind that hasn't come down to earth. Watching the swirling clouds causes a bit of dizziness, no matter how mesmerizing, so I concentrate on the aspect of the light. Morning light, the glimpse of sun, has a quality, a beauty, perhaps of promise, more stunning than the sunset. The magenta of the evening sky is a recent phenomenon, likely nothing but a chlorofluorocarbonated special effect.

As the mist leaves the lake, I can see that bright fibreglass dominates the shoreline, molded into wavy slides, paddleboats, kayaks, speedboats, loungers, and swing sets. The neighbours have actually shipped in sand to create a beach on the rocky shore, cut down the trees to create a view, to allow the sun to reach the deck, now shaded by an umbrella.

When I return with my second cup of coffee, the neighbour children are at the water making the noise of ten screaming monkeys, breaking the spell. Tomorrow, I'll get up at sunrise and force a couple hours of peace and solitude into the day. I turn my back on the frog-catching children and wish I'd brought my Discman to tune them out, never thought I'd have to create a wall of sound up here.

Daddy comes down and is asked to help, but he doesn't want to get his hands dirty, doesn't want to get his feet wet just yet. I've got to see what this guy looks like. Average. Undeserving of a piece of this paradise in his Acapulco tee-shirt. He catches me looking, so I wave, neighbourly, though I really want to pretend he doesn't exist.

"Where's Brook?" he shouts above his children.

"Still sleeping."

"Hey kids, leave the frogs alone. We'll go tubing."

They could be amused for hours catching frogs and he could go and wake his wife with a little sleepy sex, but he's suggesting speeding around the lake at nine o'clock in the morning. I sneak another look, and he's staring at me. I don't like the way he's looking. Wifely sleepy sex is out of the question. I unhook the back of my bikini top and flash him a tiny bit of tit. Perhaps if he gets turned on he'll do it, surprise her with a bit of spontaneous passion instead of taking out his boat.

When the others come down to the dock an hour later, Acapulco man and his wife are invited over for Bloody Caesars. They are the Whitmans, Rodney and Mayzie Whitman, and their children are Rod Jr. and Wally, after grandfather Whitman, not the poet, they explain.

"Philippa and I met in Acapulco," Brendan tells Rodney, pointing at his tee-shirt. "When were you there?"

"I guess it was '93, right, honey?"

"Sounds about right. Rod Jr. would have been four and Wally two. That's right, because he said his first complete sentence. Remember?"

"How can I forget. We spent the rest of the trip listening to him talk. It was so exciting."

I wish I could nudge Brendan, whisper in his ear that this is what I meant last night, that I had to postpone the era when holidays pinnacled with baby talk. He'd nod and smile and understand, and share my gratitude for the reprieve.

"That's when we were there. The year NAFTA was ratified to include the Mexicans. I was in a crappy border town for work and left for a week at a resort. There was Philippa, away from home on her own for the very first time, too fair for much sunbathing, sitting alone in the shade looking miserable."

He's not putting me down, it's true that I was miserable, and his voice contains a tenderness from the memory of taking care of me, but why does he have to mention it? My friends had all deserted me for the beach and I was burnt to a crisp from the previous day. I was so relieved to have company. Brendan introduced me to tequila shots, we played beach volleyball, rented a jeep, and he drove me around. We went to the discos each night and danced to ten-year-old music, Madonna and Michael Jackson and Prince. I was grateful for being rescued, and impressed by this sophisticated older guy who seemed to have been everywhere, had an important job, and really was a lot of fun. We even worked for the same company, and he was about to be transferred from Toronto to Cincinnati.

Why didn't I suspect that holiday romances should be left as such, turned in at the front desk with the key? People aren't really themselves on vacation because we can be whoever we feel like being. But the coincidence of it all carried me away, as did the notion of someone to take care of me. I had lovely photos of him, of us together, pinned to my cubicle wall, and I would daydream looking at them. The other women in the office would come by and look and ask how long till his arrival, tease me, tell me it was like a romance novel. We spoke on the telephone once a week, and by the time he arrived in Cincinnati two months later, I'd built him up into something of godlike proportions. I remember being surprised that he wasn't still tanned, and while his appearance was less sexy as a result, I looked harder for other qualities to compensate, qualities that really were more important than sun-kissed skin.

We became engaged after six months, married half a year later, before it all wore off. No, before I really knew him. I was so flattered that he had chosen me and viewed our marriage as a great accomplishment. I thought we shared the same goals. We did. Just different variations. I wanted to see the world, and we travelled extensively, but it wasn't the same. He worked while I saw the sights alone; we were on two separate spheres, converging for meals and sleep and not much else. So while my life expanded with each of these trips, his contracted into work. I realized his life had already peaked, at Princeton on a rowing scholarship, while mine seemed vaguely yet-to-come.

When did I first suspect? Spain? Madrid? In that square with the flea market? There was a group of tinker types hanging out, smoking hash and drinking while they put coloured braids in people's hair. I watched them for a while, one fellow in particular, and he kept staring directly into my eyes, which frightened me a little. I was afraid that if he talked to me, invited me to go somewhere with him, I would. Still, I had my hair braided just to extend my time there, to see if he'd approach. I can't quite put my finger on it, but something cracked in me, the veneer of the years. I felt the box I'd built around myself and wanted to get outside of it.

First words out of his tight little mouth Tuesday morning: "I noticed at the cottage you're getting fat, Philippa."

My response: "It's not fat, Brendan. I've ripened, like a sweet and juicy peach, from the perfect conditions of late. I think I like it, though my breasts sometimes hurt. Don't suggest a diet. It won't work, even if I tried." A single slice of toast is between us on the table, and I see it as a prop in a play-acting game. He's eyeing it also, so I reach out and score.

"Exercise, at least."

I load jam on, let it accumulate a little in the corner of my mouth before I speak.

"You have no right to say that. It's my body."

"I've heard of wives putting on weight so they won't be attractive to their partners."

I wipe the jam away with my finger, lick it suggestively.

"Have I displayed any unwillingness?"

"No, but you know I liked you the way you were. I like slim women."

You'd think I was huge. Ten pounds of new fat cushion my hips and belly and breasts, bringing me up to 125. It's the lethargy of depression doing it to me, really, lingering hormones maybe. Somehow I gather the strength to be angry rather than hurt — a recent reaction for me, and I prefer it.

"What on earth would you have thought of me when I was nine-months pregnant?"

"That's different."

"Afterwards?"

Silence. They don't think about that, do they? They think we all just deflate like a burst balloon.

"I thought we agreed on the weekend to try to make this marriage work, Brendan. If you don't want it to, tell me now, because it's tiring me out."

"Maybe you don't really want it to work. Maybe that's why you're letting yourself go."

He has no idea that I force myself each day to appear only mildly sexual so he won't freak out.

"That's really rich, Brendan. It's a horrid expression and really quite inane. Maybe you've spent some time in the pop-psychology section at that bookstore down the street. Maybe, at thirty-one, my body is finally changing into a woman's body. We're not built to be titless, hipless wonders, you know. If you don't like it, divorce me. I'll confess to insanity so you need not embarrass us both by stating weight gain as reasonable grounds."

"Why are you trying, Philippa? You really don't seem to like me much."

"How can I like you when you're always looking at me out of a corner of your eye? I've never seen an eye filled with more disdain. I don't know what to say, what to do, can't even figure out how the hell to dress anymore without it starting something. I failed you, I know you believe that. Then I hurt your feelings, or your ego maybe. How long do I have to suffer your moods for it?"

The ego bit hits a nerve that causes his face to twitch perceptibly. It is an ego thing, which is understandable, but I never thought I had the power to affect that. I thought his was as solid and massive as the CN Tower, dominating the skyline and confident of its status as the world's tallest free-standing structure.

"Can't we just try to be nice to each other, Brendan? Please? Then we'll assess things. I swear I'm not letting myself go. I'm afraid of your criticism." That's good, I think, to admit to fear, to help him recover his position. "I think I'm reaching some sort of sexual peak like they talk about in the magazines, some kind of surge of hormones. But you don't seem to like it, so I'm trying to hide it."

"That's absurd."

"It's not! It's documented. Where do you think I'm getting my ideas? Women want more sex as they get older, and men want less."

"It's absurd that I don't seem to like it. I would if it didn't seem tainted."

They really do like to keep the icons separate, Madonna and whore. It's easier for them. Too much of one and they dump their wives of twenty-five years and go running for a mistress. Too much the other way and they are threatened or something. It's curious. How's a woman to know which to be in order to get along? Where's the line drawn in the male psyche? Maybe I should read the men's mags instead of the women's, the ones about being a lad, leave them around for him to read so we're on the same track. The suggestions I've been given recently obviously aren't for him.

"Can't you try to enjoy it without thinking of me as a slut?"

"I never really thought of you as overly sexual."

"I wasn't. Now I am."

"Does it make it seem less like we're trying to make a baby?"

"Now that is truly daft!"

◆

When he leaves, I sink to hurt and cry self-pitying tears, a real jag of a cry, premenstrual in severity, and a quick check in my diary confirms it, makes me feel saner, with licence to weep. I strip and examine my body in the full-length mirror. Sure I'm more rounded, jiggle when I jump up and down. Brendan doesn't know my secret, that my added weight is a kind of comfort, a reassurance that I will not fall off the world on its next rotation. But what I am uncomfortable with is the obvious femaleness, was better with my previous androgyny, enhanced to either end of the spectrum depending on my surroundings and mood. Ever since I went off the pill, my body seems to invite men to impregnate it, screams it during ovulation, and I know when that is because I can feel it, the cyst popping and spurting a thirty-one-year-old egg down the tube in its own albumen-like substance, it too occasionally blood-spotted. I even look my best when I'm fertile, I noticed this recently, likely exude perfect pheromones for attracting a mate. This is Mother Nature's fault. No feminist there. Mother Nature is clearly part of the religious right.

Maybe there's something to the theory that women starve themselves because they're afraid of that role. Maybe that's why some of us can't enjoy it, the risk is too great. Brendan's right. It's easier when it's just sex.

He wastes no time and calls to tell me I can see his doctor that same afternoon.

I don't want to go.

"I have no cash on me."

"I told him about your status. He'll bill me. His address . . ."

◆

I watch for heavy women on the street en route to the doctor. Ample women don't walk, they throb, all butt and breast and pride. I mimic their movements and throw my shoulders back to help my breasts defy gravity. My hips oscillate and display their power with each step through the throngs of people. I don't move for them, they must get out of my way, and I walk to maximize my space on the sidewalk, the way men do.

◆

Dr. Stump is an old friend of Brendan's from high school, which is why I got in so fast. Which is why I don't want to be here. It's all a bit close. The office reminds me of the condo. Maybe that's the key, professional interior decorators creating the look of a safe world. Dr. Stump shakes my hand vigorously, tells me to call him Harry without a thought that I might find this funny. Brendan told him I was depressed, told him his suspicions, no doubt, everything except to check me for AIDS. I ask him for that, to shock him, to embarrass Brendan if the confidentiality pact is broken. On a roll with that idea, I ask him to check me for pregnancy also, pronounce it as though it is the disease to be concerned about. Five minutes later, I leave with a requisition for the tests, a bottle of Prozac he keeps for women just like me, and a follow-up appointment in a month, to see how I'm faring. I was told to stop taking the pills if I experienced any psychotic episodes, or if I found myself being nasty and irrational. I was told to stop taking them if either of the tests was positive, which struck me as ludicrous because you'd think I'd really need a little help then. I was told to give his regards to Dan.

I awaken with the idea that a little cookery will lift my spirits more than the pills. I'll take one later, I promise, a tad wary of joining the Prozac Nation. Surely a bout of creativity is a better remedy. As I lie in bed, I think of how to ritualize the day, spread it out in my mind like the banquet in which it will culminate. I plan my time hour by hour and make an intricately itemized list of ingredients and details of garnishes.

I need a name for the day, an accessory to match my plans and mood. Perhaps . . . Felipitta. I repeat it aloud in the shower several times before settling on a pronunciation that stresses the first *i* and the *a*. It works, matches, fits in so many different ways, crossing flip and felicity. I lather my body with sandalwood soap and reach for a razor, then remember my role and check to see if the length of my underarm hair is sufficiently Italianate.

Felipitta's chosen dress is from Benetton, of course, though it really looks like any old North American dress. The tag is enough to make me feel Italian. As I stroll down Cumberland on a perfect, arid, and sunny morning, the street is transformed by the Three Tenors on my Discman into Rome's *Via veneto*. I wish I knew a little Italian, enough to order a cappuccino, at least. My first stop is the coffee shop — the café — where tables are aligned all facing the street, European style, because the true essence of such places in other parts of the world is to watch and be watched, not conversation. The arrangement is civilized and democratic, doesn't discriminate against solitary patrons. I write a list while fashionable store clerks pass on their way to tend to the specific luxuries inside their shops. Most of the men are Italian, in Italian suits and shoes, and move with grace, as though their apparel is automated, wired to control their movements. Wouldn't that be a useful invention, more so than the Japanese aromatherapy suits I've heard about, designed to alleviate stress but worn and shimmied in to mask odours from late nights in smoky bars. The thought makes me smile, and rather than waste it, and the good feelings, I bestow it upon the men as they size me up. I want to see saleswomen, to see how they move in their Italian fashions, but it's mostly my neighbours out walking their dogs through the multi-terrain park, around the 650-tonne imported Muskoka rock. Topiary toy poodles and Pomeranians and Jack Russells: condo pets. If only the need to piss and poop on oriental rugs could be bred out of them, genetically modified in a useful application of the science, they'd be perfect. I'd like a little dog for company, but can't imagine walking around with a plastic bag to pick up after them, throwing the poo in a public waste container.

The coffee is rich and strong and lightly flavoured by a dusting of cinnamon. My schedule allows time for a single cup, though I want another, haven't had a decent coffee in a month. Consulting the day, I squeeze in an espresso between 2. shopping and 3. walk home.

◆

Little Italy doesn't live up to its quaint street signs and boot-shaped lights. The types of shops I'd anticipated are absent and it is little more than a street of trendy restaurants. Where are the friendly greengrocers and butchers? The women in black gossiping on the sidewalk? Further west there is a supermarket, so I resign myself to it, and while I crave a total experience for the day, it's a relief to find an orderly, well-stocked place to shop, and it does have an authentic Italian bakery in one corner. I'm confused by the number of different types of olive oil, not just the brands but the degrees of virginity, wonder why there aren't different degrees of virginity for women, like if you don't reach orgasm it's not quite gone, or after six months of abstinence it returns in part, not just in increased levels of desire.

It is more expeditious to make purchases all at once, so I have plenty of time for my espresso. I choose the terrace of Bar Italia and ask the waiter where the Italian shops are located.

"The rent's too high for them now. They closed up."

"Are there any other ethnic neighbourhoods, specific ones, and real, not just theme parks like this?"

"Sure. Chinatown, the Danforth, though it's getting much like here. Little India's probably the best, filled with saris and incense and curly-toed slippers."

"Where is it?"

"Along Gerrard. Take the College car to Hiawatha Avenue. Ask the driver, he'll call it out for you."

I write the directions down on the back of my list.

"Kensington, of course."

I look up. "What's that?"

"An outdoor market. Best selection in the city, from all over the world."

I jot it down also, but the curly-toed slipper place will be next.

"Would you mind recommending a good Italian wine? Not for now, one I can buy."

"Sure. But what about grappa?"

"Is that a brand?"

"You don't know grappa? Mamma mia!" he says, to amuse. "Come with me and I'll get you a little taste. You must choose from the bottle that you find most appealing. The bottles are each like works of art. Italians. Even their bottles have to have style."

"You're not Italian?"

"Me? Not at all."

Felipitta smiles at this.

"Why did I expect to find authentic Italian everything around here?"

"I can be more authentic than any Italian you'll meet in this neighbourhood. So which of those bottles appeals to you?"

Felipitta examines the gallery of long-necked coloured glass vessels on a shelf.

"The blue one in the middle," I say.

"The señora has taste."

The grappa is sweeter than I'd anticipated, and strong.

"So it's an aperitif?"

"Digestive. And an aphrodisiac. It's similar to perfume if you sprinkle it on your body. It combines with your individual flavour."

"I'm trying to spice up my marriage a little. That might be a fine idea."

"Damn. I was going to suggest it myself."

What fun to flirt like this. What a relief to know it's still possible.

"If it doesn't work on him, I'll bring you the remainder. What's your name?"

"Pasquale."

"That's an Italian name."

"Of course. It's my work name. If I meet you outside of work, I'll tell you my social name."

"My name today is Felipitta."

"Pleasure, Felipitta. Come back, even if the grappa is successful."

"Thanks. I will."

◆

I think the need for finding ways to instill order is a particularly female quality. Not the need for order itself, but the creation of opportunity and the satisfaction from the doing. Men, on the other hand, go straight for control. That's what I heard about female addiction to the computer game Tetris. Putting everything in order. In cooking terms, the prep is called *mise en place*: put in place. It has become a noun, a thing. Here's my *mise en place*, and to look at it in such a way is satisfying. If only momentarily, it applies to my life, and is inspiration to achieve order all around.

I haven't really cooked anything interesting in months. It's all been meat and potatoes, and Brendan insists on barbecuing that anyway. Even at the cottage, when I was desperate to distance myself for a bit, the men manned the barbecue. I'd challenged them for the privilege, and the pair of them had launched into some sort of thesis about primal urges and open flames and how it is a defining moment of summer for them, an event.

Fresh basil exudes such a strong aroma, it has perfumed the air in the kitchen even before I've begun cooking. The smells will change and mix and I will use them, not taste, to guide me. The sense of smell is more accurate, is an essential part of taste, really. That's why heavy congestion hampers both. So I learned in cooking class last year. Ma taught me to cook with my eyes for determining readiness rather than relying on a timer or thermometer, to use my hands to feel the proper consistency of bread and pastry dough. She would be appalled by my bread machine, by all my appliances that keep hands clean and removed from the process. She wouldn't believe a machine could possibly know if a texture was right. To her it's an art, and variables such as heat and humidity and the very nature of the wheat crop must be taken into consideration.

I feel brave and confident, so use the recipes as outlines really, modify them by adding extra garlic, more basil and oregano, because I have fresh and they call for pinches of the dried crap from shaker jars. I rinse and chop and mix and wash up as I go, sip on a slightly currenty Pinot Noir every now and then.

Before Brendan arrives home, I shake out my hair, get back in my dress, and apply a few dabs from a tester of perfume scammed from a store earlier. The clerks don't like to give those out if you don't buy something, like it's some kind of skin off their backs, but are understanding of women who say they must have husbandly approval before committing to a fragrance. The trick is to act as though you'd buy a hundred-dollar bottle in a flash, but are playing the game by the correct rules. The key is not to allow them to intimidate you, to demonstrate a precise aura of haughtiness and rudeness.

The enjoyable day, a little risqué flirtation, the leisurely cooking and accomplishment of creation have all put me in fine form, and I'm even looking forward to seeing him, experiencing his reaction, perhaps a scrap of praise. A step towards getting along. The tension is gone and I do feel a little bit in control, think I can stop the nasty thoughts about him because it really isn't his fault that I've been so anxious.

When I hear him come in, I call out a cheery greeting.

"Sit and relax while I get you a scotch. I've had the best day."

I bring his drink, then kiss his cheek.

"No, wait." I redo my movements and kiss him on both sides. "We're in Milano this evening, and you can call me Felipitta, ease your way into being nice to me."

"You really have flipped, haven't you?"

"A little, yes, but it's fun." I smile at him and stroke his cheek. "How was your day?"

"Hectic."

I go to the kitchen to check on things, call out something pleasant and instructive. Constructive, not destructive. Repeat.

"Will you pour the wine? It's a Barolo and should've breathed twenty minutes, but it's only been about ten."

"Barolo?"

"Do you have any desire to take a wine-tasting course with me?"

"Not really."

"No. I realized today how poorly this kitchen is equipped. If you enjoy your meal tonight, might you consider a few purchases?"

"Don't see why not. It looks as though we'll be here longer than I thought. Maybe even long-term."

My hand brushes the side of the oven.

"Damn. Ow. I burnt myself."

"Aren't there oven mitts even?"

"They're useless. A useless invention. And highly flammable besides."

I run my hand under cold water. He's happy about this, not about to ask my opinion because he doesn't want to be challenged on it.

"Sit down. Everything's ready."

I light two tapers and carry them to the table. Brendan tastes the wine, looks at the label.

"Nice."

"They're very knowledgeable at the Vintages section in the Manulife Centre." Where are these statements coming from? I remind myself of a television advert. There's a good new usage. Advert your life, turn it inside out, into something happy and pretty and obtainable, absent of all traces of controversy. This is what he wants, what he needs. This is what I have to give him.

Felipitta had prepared cannelloni, alternately stuffed with a three-mushroom, three-cheese filling, and minced veal with sun-dried tomatoes. Both swim in a vodka-tomato cream sauce. The plates are dusted with finely chopped oregano and basil.

When I bring the food to the table and sit down, Brendan raises his glass in my direction. "Thank you," he says, and I detect sincerity.

"My pleasure. I enjoyed doing it."

The tastes of the meal seem to complement the wine more than the wine complements the food. It's the added bonus of using smell as a guide. When you finally taste, it is surprising, a treat for the cook. Overstimulated taste buds won't appreciate all the subtleties, the layers and locations of the flavours.

"This is amazing, Phillie. I can't decide which I like better, the mushroom or the beef."

"*Funghi.*"

"Eh?"

"Italian for mushroom. I prefer the *funghi* one. The other's veal, actually."

"Is there more?"

"Loads. Give me your plate."

I finish my own meal with satisfaction and watch jealously as Brendan uses the last piece of focaccia to wipe his plate clean.

"It's better than going out. More intimate," I say.

He says: "I like going out."

We end the meal with sour cherry pie and vanilla Häagen-Dazs, our favourite, the pie straight from the oven as a nod to Ma's old-fashioned advice.

I clear the table, not before refilling both our glasses. Clearly my husband will have to be a little bit drunk before he'll fully relax. Clearly I must be as well, so I take my time with the dishes to allow us both an opportunity to digest and finish our wine.

I suggest we sit on the balcony for a bit, bring the bottle of grappa with me, and offer it to Brendan to open.

"Ever had grappa?" I ask.

"Never heard of it."

"It's made from leftover grape skins."

I settle in my chair and place my feet on Brendan's upper thigh.

"Like it?"

"Sure."

"Let's do this every night from now on."

"Some nights I don't feel like such a big production. It was great, though," he adds, adverting also, or perhaps that word isn't accurate if you're not faking it as much as I am.

"How long do you think we'll be here now?"

"It's tough to say. Once the welfare thing is finished, we might get the health-care consulting contract."

"So, more than six months?"

"More like a year." He sneaks a look at me and I smile. "At least."

"I do want to make the most of it, Brendan. I think I can be a little happier if I just try a bit harder." I slide one foot down a little. Brendan sips his grappa, says nothing.

"Do you think anyone bothers to look up here when they pass by?"

"I shouldn't think so."

I contrive an innocent flash of my underwear as I get up from my chair. I must become Felipitta again, so I sit sideways in his lap, dip a finger in my glass, and spread the grappa around his lips before kissing them.

"Mmm. It takes on a whole different flavour like that. You try."

As he finishes, Felipitta licks his fingertip, then reaches for his hand to bring the whole finger into her mouth. He kisses her with more passion than I thought he could ever summon, so I continue, undo his shirt, and draw a line from his throat to his navel. While in the vicinity, I begin to undo his trousers.

"Let's go inside," he says.

Hooray for grappa.

But what's this? He's doing up his pants, ending it. How am I supposed to react to this? Shards of fatigue, bitterness, and embarrassment fight to pierce my composure as I watch him move through the patio doors, see him pick up the remote, and recline on the couch. Do I actually have to compete with the television? Big breath, join him on the couch.

He flips through the twenty-five channels on free trial offer. I could either cancel the whole package or sabotage the television tomorrow. I don't recognize anything worth watching, but he stops at the all-news station and commentary about the latest conflict. They're still careful not to call it a war, like they actually believe it can be a conflict without casualties, like a blow job isn't sex, like not inhaling doesn't count. No wonder that poor woman agreed to the cigar, she was having to compete with so much more than a television, and an odd sort of logic, to figure out what might actually work to enthrall the man.

What part of myself do I offer up for humiliation? Do I press on or give up and be happy if he suddenly remembers I'm willing in the middle of the night when it awakens for the john? I don't even know where to start, what particular little tricks to pull out to get his attention. Is it possible he has determined it must be about conception and nothing else, and is trying to bribe me?

The TV will surely bore him before the next set of commercials, and he'll remember, realize pleasure is sitting at his feet. Maybe if I just rub them a little.

"That tickles," he says, and pulls them away.

They stink anyway.

June 5

The draught in the afternoon sun had made her a little drowsy, so she stripped off her slip and lay down for a nap, "a siesta," she thought, naps being for toddlers and old folk in her mind. A sultry hot breeze reached through the open window and caressed her naked body, made her think of Tommy; and as she fell into sleep, she drifted away from her irritation about being abandoned, post-poodle, once again.

She was crawling across the floor, slowly, so as to be unnoticed, moving to a strange and colourful music playing only in her mind. When she reached his feet, she began to lick softly between his toes. Her tongue moved up his leg to his hipbone, but the gentle kisses and bites created no response, only a trail of wetness and occasional small red welts. When he finally groaned in recognition of her efforts, she awakened at once.

Nova knew adolescent boys had nocturnal emissions — wet dreams — didn't know it was possible for women.

"Mind fuck," she thought. "That's what it really is, what the expression should refer to."

She wondered if this was a common phenomenon: the principle behind virtual sex, which she'd recently read about and dismissed as a form of pornography, unlikely to satisfy, but perhaps deserving of renewed consideration. Nova let her mind run with the idea that constant access to satisfaction would eliminate occasional lapses in judgment. If the results were repeatable by force of will — an erotic suggestion before sleep took over — she might achieve it on a daily basis. She wondered if courses existed, instruction booklets or self-help guides. *Orgasmic Dreaming*: surely a bestseller. Then again, it could simply be this particular man, the heady freedom of anonymity or the naughty feeling for running away from home at its root. She hoped it was one of the latter because she didn't think she should love someone like Tommy.

Her own stupidity slapped her awake, and she finally laughed at herself. "Love has nothing to do with this, you spacer. Get that through your thick head. You can use a friend, or a real stooping. Full stop." Nova realized she could likely walk out her door and within an hour find someone to take care of her needs.

❖

More pressing for a woman like Mrs. Philippa Maria Donahue were food, linen, and a cappuccino to chase away the guilty dregs of a boozy head. In her earlier explorations, Nova had discovered a store that could almost be called a supermarket because of its shopping carts. Not ten steps through the entrance and a compact old man, denied any illusion of height by a Greek fisherman's cap pushed down around his ears, hollered at her and scuttled quickly towards her, calling out, "Lady. Lady."

He frightened her, even though the address was adequately respectful, and Nova wondered if the store had restricted access, was about to close, or wasn't really open despite the appearance of being so. Coffee really should have been the priority to eliminate this high-grade confusion. He pointed to a row of cardboard boxes at the front of the store and told her to put her bag there. It held fresh bread, expensive French Brie, and a tin of smoked mussels for her dinner.

"Someone might take it," she said, offended by the suggestion that she was a potential shoplifter. "I'm not going to steal anything."

"No. I watch it."

Nova reluctantly set her bag in the box farthest from the door, fearing an absent-minded shopper would mistake it for her own. She'd be stuck with liver or pigs' trotters, any number of leftover body parts, or, ooooh, those creamy non-smoker lungs seen suspended like clouds in a window with the intestines below, a sight that caused her to run across the street. Organs and intestines were to be avoided now as potential speakers of directives and truths. But even if a bag held more acceptable meat, it would still require a stove she did not have, and so she tried to hurry through the aisles. Speed was stymied by the store's unusual arrangement of goods. An odd sort of person had imposed their sense of order, had somehow thought to put rat traps beside pots and pans, aluminum foil with microwaveable foodstuffs, pickles and jam side by each as though on some long-ago pantry shelf. Half the store was devoted to other essentials: linen, clothing, imperfect pantyhose and underwear at a third the price in a regular store.

She rummaged through piles of sheets and towels, searching for tastefully solid colours, found writing paper mysteriously, but in fact conveniently, next to toiletries, else she might have forgotten underarm deodorant and disposable razors. At the last moment she added a sun hat to prevent the heat from going to her head as it had done earlier, and a half-dozen nylon floral panties in sickly sweet shades. The panties were iffy, possible producers of a yeast infection, but there were no cotton options. When she reached the line-up, the funny little man materialized and motioned her over to a free register. She paused to confirm his intent, pointed at her cleavage, which was, after all, at the root of the preferred customer service.

"Thank you, lady. See your bag is there. I like you, lady. Come back and see me soon."

Nova smiled winningly at the dwarfish man as though this was more of what Tommy meant: friendly merchants who would come to know her and stop demanding that she leave her bags with those of the riff-raff.

Directly across from her epiphanic site on Fish Street, an empty bench enclosed in a penalty box of a patio promised a desirable combination of solitude and stimuli from the street. Inside, a few customers at the bar spoke hurried Portuguese, and Nova recognized two of them as vocally competing fish-mongers from neighbouring shops. She'd seen them earlier, heard them shouting prices for live crabs crawling on the side-walk, but Nova had thought they were arguing and on the verge of fisticuffs. She'd stepped carelessly into the street to avoid their aggression and was nearly struck by a passing cyclist.

She ignored these particular new neighbours, not wanting to encourage their leers, either here or on the other side of street, and asked the man behind the counter if he had any special coffee.

"Do I know you?"

"I don't think so. I'm new here." The question was curious. "Nova."

"What sort of special coffee, Nova?"

"Any kind."

The men eyed her, looked at one another, and shrugged. Nova assumed she seemed ditzy, that of course this grotty establishment wouldn't have designer coffee.

Back outside, she set her notepaper on the table, lit a cigarette, and took a sip from the Styrofoam cup. The brandy was strong and made her eyes water and crinkle up in irritation because she recognized that more booze was not what she needed. Through the window, the men watched and laughed and gave the thumbs-up. She'd never considered ridicule as being a direct route to feeling accepted, but here it seemed to be, so she took no offence.

When she picked up her pen, its shape felt unfamiliar and her initial handwriting looked forced. She never wrote letters anymore; all correspondence was through e-mail, and her penmanship had suffered as a result. She'd change that by producing beautiful, tactile letters from now on.

Dear Brendan,

I haven't gone home for the weekend. I can't explain it very well, but I needed to escape. I'm 31 years old and don't know who I am or what I want to do for the rest of my life. I only know I don't wish to be limited to being someone's wife and someone else's mother, and that's exactly what you seem to want from me. I've been away from you for only two days and already feel like a different person. You probably wouldn't even recognize me, and if you did, I don't think you'd like what you saw. I do. I realize this seems abrupt, and I don't expect you to understand because I don't fully understand it myself yet. I've been so anxious lately, I had to do something for myself, find some way to stimulate myself. I'm desperately afraid of living a mediocre life, of waking up when I'm middle-aged and realizing that I've achieved nothing but mediocrity. I sent my folks a telegram, so you need not contact them. I'll call in a little while, when I sort things out a bit more.

Philippa

She put the letter in an envelope and addressed it formally, sealed it without regret and only a flash of thought for the consequences. It was against her territorial rule to deliver it herself, so Nova scouted for a leisurely pedestrian who might serve as a courier. Most of the people were couples, or families, or of a different colour than her own and therefore unapproachable in Philippa's mind. As she searched the crowds she noticed most of the couples were of mixed race, homogeneity being the rarity, and it challenged her image of the order of the world. She noticed many belly buttons best left covered, hairy ass cracks, and orange-peel thighs, caught herself staring and averted her eyes across the street to a mural of a Greek fisherman. The paint was peeling around the mouth, giving him a rabid frothing look, and she quickly looked away in the event that it too would speak — a likely culprit if ever she saw one.

Finally, a couple of squeegee kids ambled down the middle of the road with an unleashed pit bull and Nova wondered if she could trust them. Brendan had told her that squeegee kids were notoriously violent and shifty, repeatedly warned her not to open her window to them for fear they'd snatch her purse. Motivated by spite, she chose them as messengers.

"Oye!" she shouted, trying to sound like a recent film version of young and aimless youths. "Do either of you want to make ten bucks?"

"To do what?"

"Deliver a letter for me."

"Just a letter?"

"Uh-huh."

"Why's it worth a tenner then?"

"It's a letter to my husband and I don't want to see him. It's worth ten bucks for you to deliver it and keep mum about where I am."

"Where's he?"

"Yorkville."

"No way. We ain't going up there."

Nova bribed them with a drink, and the boys grinned and told her to get them a couple of pints. They tied up the dog and quickly slipped into the box, sat with their backs to the window. The owner wasn't altogether concerned about minors, but it was not to be flaunted — out of respect. They introduced themselves as Lucky and Cerberus, Cerb for short, and Nova felt an immediate kinship with them for their assumed identities, asked about the origin of their chosen names.

"I figure if people call me Lucky all day, every day, eventually I might be."

"Cerberus is the coolest mythological beast, the most wicked. If I could be anything, I'd be him. Has a ring to it, don't it?"

Nova nodded. "Who was he again?"

"Fuckin' three-headed dog guarding the gates of hell. Got ripped in the mythological fame department."

Though he only had one head, she thought the alias fit, was onomatopoeic, in fact, confusing "sounds like it is" for "acts like it is," as the guardian of the gates seemed to have fleas. Nova Philip had not yet been educated in the subtler indications of a fondness for junk, the whole-body-itch this boy was experiencing.

Lucky said, "So what's the deal with your old man?"

"I just don't want a scene."

"What? He's beating on you or something? We can deal with that too if you want. Make it twenty — ba da bing, ba da boom!"

"I'm a bit embarrassed to say, but it's just the opposite. He thinks I've gone to visit my family for the weekend. The letter tells him I've run away — to join the circus, so to speak."

"Cool!" said Lucky.

"So what are you?" asked Cerb.

"What do you mean?"

"Your circus act? Lion tamer? Clown? Bearded woman?"

They had a good laugh at that last one.

"I hadn't really thought about it, but *definitely* not bearded woman."

"Not glamorous, right? You want one of those sexy little sequiny outfits like the trapeze girls, flashing your undies at the kiddies."

It was ironic to her that Cerb felt entitled to use the word "kiddies" when he wasn't more than sixteen himself. He also could have passed for "Dog Boy" even without the scratching and the canine nickname, and Nova might have suggested as much in retaliation if she hadn't needed the favour.

"I'd swallow knives. Or fire," said Lucky.

"But those are just illusions," Nova pointed out.

"I'd do it for real. Or be a super-masochist and nail my dick to a board and hang from it."

"That's sick," she said, disgusted by the thought, the pain.

"You saw the film?"

"What film?"

"*Sick*."

"No."

"That's what the guy did — performances — filmed it all."

"Why?"

"I suppose so people would stop calling it sick."

"That's a bit extreme."

"It's extreme times, isn't it."

Nova considered whether the times would ever reach such extremes. Couldn't fathom it. Decided not likely.

"So you want us to give the letter to your daddy in person, or slip it under the door?" Lucky continued.

She wanted to instruct them to present themselves, for the shock value, for the story they would relate to her about the look on his face, a yarn she could then spin to entertain a table at the Plate the next time she found herself without anything to say. It wouldn't be right, though, to use them in that way, so she told them, "Slip it under the door. He'd be the type to identify you to the police."

"Ahhh. You didn't say anything about that."

"Yeah. That'll cost you an extra fiver. Call it danger pay. Our kind's not exactly popular these days."

"Okay, but I'm not paying you until you come back with proof that you actually did it."

"What kind of proof?"

"I don't know. Describe the hallway to me, or something."

"You'll be here?"

"Yes."

"Why should we trust you if you won't trust us?"

"Do I look anything but trustworthy?"

"To who? Others exactly like you, sure. But us and you, we're of different tribes."

Nova assumed her wholesome Midwestern appearance was universally recognizable as trustworthy, transcendent of the fear of the unknown, the strange. These disheveled, pierced, and tattooed boys were the untrustworthy. She doubted they even trusted each other.

"Do you know Tommy?" she tried. "He seems to know everyone around here."

They both nodded.

"I'm a friend of his. You can track me down through him."

"Like he's super-trustworthy-man or something."

"Yeah, you got that reference in writing?"

"He led me to believe this was the kind of place where people might help each other out. Never mind. I'll find someone else who wants to make some quick cash."

The threat of the money disappearing into someone else's pocket was sufficient to end the game.

"Okay, but you better be here."

As soon as they were off, Nova experienced some mild anxiety now that her proclamation was en route, but it was impossible to sit in front of the bar in solitude, and her mind was soon diverted. A 5 PM jazz jam attracted a gang of punks and she felt slightly intimidated by them. They ignored her initially, then glared, but once it was apparent the treatment wouldn't drive her off the limited real estate, they sussed her out with a few direct questions and acknowledged that her

recent decampment sanctioned her presence on the bench for
a short while.

A fleeting adolescent attraction to a similar crowd — their
fashion in particular — had cemented her banishment to
what she called St. Margaret's School for Wicked Girls. As she
sat among the punks now, she wondered what her life would
be had she actually joined them, defied her parents rather
than cave under the weight of their love and concern and dis-
appointment. She might very well be hanging around a similar
establishment somewhere else in the world, with a different
sort of husband. Time constricted in her mind and tricked her
into imagining the past sixteen years could be reclaimed, that
she was at that very moment where she should be, where she
would have been.

Nova listened to a few dull exchanges between passing
couples and was reminded of how she and Brendan spoke,
might speak, if they were here, together.

"How much did we pay for zucchinis yesterday?"

"Just one more stop and then we'll go."

"Quit your whining or you can wait in the car."

This scolding made Nova shiver, though it had been
directed at a child, and a sweet relief supplanted her unease
about the letter.

People stopped tentatively at the door and wished that
either their schedules or prurience permitted a cocktail in the
midst of Saturday chores. They eyed the dangerous-looking
crowd out front and moved along. Nova Philip felt mildly
superior, thought, "Look at me, I've thrown off the chains of
your Protestant work ethic, your guilt." She switched back to
draught to entrench the belief that she really had, and struck
up a conversation with the straightest-looking female on the

patio about the best place to buy appropriate footwear for the sloppy market terrain. She knew shoes were always a good topic with women, even of different tastes. Her sandals were already ruined, soiled from the earlier spillage and stinking with dog shit compressed in their minimal treading. She wanted Docs, like this one was wearing — Cherry Docs, she remembered — because she thought they'd make her feel braver, more confident than she did at that moment. But the boots were becoming a rare commodity, no longer a viable export to Canada, and she'd be best off at a second-hand store called Black Market. They had a good selection still, already nicely seasoned with attitude.

Cerberus and Lucky returned and tried to extort additional cash, threatened to tie her up and tell her husband where to come find her, told her to think of it as reverse kidnapping: pay them a ransom to keep herself free. Nova wasn't certain these boys weren't serious and for a moment was concerned for her freedom.

"What's wrong with you, anyway? You don't like the high life up there?"

"It felt constricting all of a sudden."

"No shit."

Dan Donahue used to think his wife was a sensible woman. It was one of the reasons he married her. Apart from being insensible, her current actions were selfish: he didn't have time for this sort of silliness, this obvious ploy to get a little attention. Though he knew he'd been ignoring her — not ignoring really, he was just so incredibly busy — he had thought she'd accepted what was required of him.

He reread the letter, looking for clues between the lines to explain her tantrum. "You probably wouldn't recognize me, and if you did, I don't think you'd like what you saw. I do." What the hell was that supposed to mean? A new haircut? Had she spent too much money on another shopping spree and was afraid to face him?

When he'd heard from her parents, he'd immediately called the people they knew in Toronto, without revealing the nature of his call, hoping one of them would slip up somehow and give Philippa away. They were simply puzzled at his seemingly pointless conversation. He believed he knew the company she kept, because it was the same company he kept, but she could easily have met one of those lingering old feminist types who had convinced her she had a bad lot.

He now called Harry Stump at home to ask if Philippa had disclosed anything that might enlighten him. Harry maintained the doctor-patient privilege, suggested Prozac might be the wrong drug, that a number of women had similar reactions, a soaring level of self-confidence belying their true nature.

Her reason would come back soon enough, he decided, once she got this out of her system, whatever it was. He thought he could encourage that process and first thing Monday morning would go to their bank and close the account.

Instead of attending Mass on Sunday, Nova returned to the supermarket for some cleaning products, having discovered the bathroom she shared with the two other roomers did less than meet her aesthetic requirements. Cleanliness being next to godliness, she assumed He would understand her absence.

The old guy stood outside because he no longer *really* worked there, just showed up each day to participate. Three subsequent generations took care of business now, but he still thought of it as his store, with his name on it, the original, started from nothing but a couple of crates on the sidewalk fifty years earlier.

"Lady! You come to see me. I'm waiting for you here all morning. How are you today?"

"I'm well, thank you. How are you?"

"Old. But I still know a pretty girl." He followed Nova inside and down the aisles, pretended to straighten cans and boxes as they went.

"Come," he said, when she was through, and once again led her to an unused cash register, gave her a small pat on the ass as he did so.

When she passed him her money, he grabbed her hand and held it a moment. Nova glanced down and noticed the numbers, still vivid, an obscene green like absinthe mixed milky with time and flesh.

"I like you, lady. See you tomorrow."

She felt unclean, not because of his touch, but from the sudden proximity of a horror she seldom thought of. Of course she'd seen all the movies about the subject and once knew a Jewish boy whose grandparents had been in a camp, but that was so long ago, before she was old enough to have to consider all of the implications.

"People have lives," Tommy had said. He hadn't said how she was supposed to react to such a life, how she could possibly be a part of that. Humour these possibly senile affronts to her butt? Exhibit kindness? Support this enterprise?

She went in search of Tommy to ask him about it, in and

out of various bars and cafés and clothing stores. All she knew of where he lived was that it was on Augusta/Vegetable and was kind of a half-house, the most decrepit on the street, the missing half destroyed by a fire some time back and replaced by a bunker-like building. He said he liked the way it seemed cut off, said it felt private and adequately shabby to be homey. At any rate, she wasn't altogether comfortable with the thought of just dropping in on him, so headed in the direction of the Plate to wait for him to turn up.

He noticed her from his rooftop perch where he was feeding a large bird of prey in a homemade cage.

"Looking good, porn-star girl," he shouted. Nova shook her head at his persistent ribbing and cast her eyes about for where he was located.

It took an additional "Up here!" for Nova to raise her sights in his direction, and she waved.

"Can I talk to you?" she called from the middle of the road.

"Come on up. The door's open."

Tommy shared his apartment with a sculptor friend, Dino, and the living room was strewn with paints and canvas and half-finished scrimshaw. Someone's discarded mantel framed hell-flames painted on the wall, and the traditional place for clocks and family photos was covered with small stone carvings instead.

"Grab a beer if you want," he called to her.

Nova did, even though it was not quite noon, climbed through the window and sat on a broken kitchen chair.

"Welcome to the Alcazar. This here is Freddie the Falcon."

"What are you doing with a falcon?"

"Hunting. He's great at keeping the rat and pigeon problem at bay."

"That can't be legal."

Tommy shrugged.

"He hunts at night. A few cats go missing, no one knows why, blame the poor folks in need of a little meat. The shit hawks are out of control, ditto the rats, so it's really a public health service. Besides, they're an endangered species. They allow a family of them to nest under the neon S at the Sheraton Centre."

Nova examined the bird and was unnerved by its assessing eye. It seemed to size her own up, as though it would like nothing better than to peck them out.

"What up?" he said, as he tossed the falcon a chunk of flesh.

"Why do you talk like that?"

"Street talk. Keeping hep to things. You talk the talk and walk the walk and people trust you." He glanced at Nova and added, "But you gotta have the finesse to pull it off, otherwise you're nailed as a poser." He finished his beer and crumpled the can in a near-simultaneous motion, belched loudly, and said, "What's on your mind?"

"Manners," she thought immediately, then reminded herself she was trying to ignore manners and conventions and rules.

"What do you know about the man in the supermarket up the street?"

"Which one?"

"The oldest one, with the tattoo."

"Nothing really, why?"

"It struck me that that was what you were talking about when you said people have lives."

"Well, it's a bit over the top, but sure, that's what I meant."

"What am I supposed to do about it?"

"Do? Start showing a little regard for the folks around you, that's what you're supposed to do. Stop thinking about yourself as the centre of the universe and put your life in perspective."

"It frightens me."

"Maybe that's just the point." He left her to consider this as he went for another beer.

Fright was not quite the point Nova was interested in. Fear was what she hoped to leave behind in all its choking limiting manifestations.

"In what perspective do you place your life?" she asked upon his return.

Tommy contemplated the question while he drank his beer, formulated the words to his personal manifesto, and launched into an explanation that any great era of change, any new artistic movement is accompanied by shifting levels of tolerance for what is new. Tolerance develops in the presence of horror; more accurately, the awareness of horror, because it's always present, and what is truly important rises to the surface to snuff out the petty. All great artistic expression arises from horror, not beauty as some imagine. Anyone can capture beauty; art should be chaotic, ugly, disturbing, reflecting the soul of the world.

"It takes a great artist to capture that, to endure it, actually," he concluded.

This was an opportunity to get in her own insult, and she jumped, hoping it would lessen his intimidating effect on her.

"So when's your next show?"

"I've been preoccupied lately."

"Trying to get off crack?"

"Who told you about that? I'll kill him."

Nova was pleased with herself for intuiting this aspect of his life, and told him nicely, "I was there Friday night, remember. It wasn't difficult to figure out."

"I haven't done rock in three years."

"But you still crave it."

"Yeah, I crave it. I think sometimes I always will."

"What's the attraction?"

"Power."

"What, you don't feel powerful without it?"

"Course not."

"And you preach to me about perspective?"

"I don't preach about anything."

"You do so. You call me girlie-girl, tell me to get a real life. My life's a hell of a lot more real than some crack addict's."

"Please. Ain't nothin' more real than kickin'. And girlie-girl happens to be the highest compliment I bestow. Didn't you hear? It's great to be a girl again. Thank the dykes for that one. I'm only trying to make you realize that not everyone has a cozy, pretty life. Few do, in all reality, and fewer still have any real power over their lives."

"Am I supposed to feel responsible for that? Practise that pathetic middle-class guilt or something?"

"Not guilt."

"What then?"

"Recognize where you belong."

"Not here. Is that what you think?"

"The level of tolerance is high around here because everyone has experienced some sort of shit. If you are surrounded by shit, it stops smelling so bad. Sometimes it even smells sweet."

"And you think I'll hate the smell?"

"And Bingo was his name-o."

"How do you know what I've experienced?"

"Your face. It's blank." He leaned forward with an out-stretched finger, gently touched between her eyebrows. "Except for one tiny crease, just there. I wonder what caused that little beauty mark."

"A difficult decision," she said.

"What?"

"Never mind."

Tommy shook his head. "See what I mean? You can't even admit to your own shit. There are two types of people in the Market: locals and tourists, participants and observers. You're a tourist, doll."

"Why are you so condescending towards me?"

"I'm not. Sheesh. You don't get it, do you? It's a simple fact, nothing else. I'm only trying to spare you grief. Trust me. You'll freak around here. In fact, I was shocked to see you yesterday, assumed you'd have gone back to the suburbs."

It was Nova's turn to get another beer, and as she approached the window she turned to look him straight in the eye and said quite forcefully, "You know nothing about me, mister know-it-all, see-it-all. You don't even know my real name." With that, she struggled awkwardly through the window, losing a bit of the high ground to clumsiness.

"Get me another while you're in there, would you?" Tommy called after her.

Nova shook the can a little as she carried it across the living room, tossed it gently out the window at him before climbing through again.

"So tell me," he said.

"Tell you what?"

The beer sprayed directly in his face and foamed down the side of the can.

"Fuck!" he said, licking beer from his hand before wiping his face. "You did that deliberately, didn't you?"

Nova shook her head and laughed until her eyes watered. "I swear, it was an accident."

"Right. Whatever. Very funny. Don't ever waste my beer like that again."

"Fine. Don't ever accuse me of being suburban again."

"Hit a nerve, did I?"

"Look," she said, wiping her eyes, adopting a conciliatory tone. "All I want is to find a little room for myself for a change. I think I can do it here, that there's that kind of space."

Tommy rolled his eyes.

"It's what I was talking about — the tolerance. You can do pretty much what you want. Work or don't work and no one will say a word until you become a pest about it. Drink all day. Swim in the kiddie pool if you don't look and act like a potential pedophile. Walk around in your pajamas because the Chinese do. It's acceptable for me to have no dough, to be committed to my painting — out there it's not. Creativity and oddity are seen as diseases to be cured, and you're just a bum until your pieces hang in the two or three acceptable galleries and you're invited to cocktail parties."

He paused to look sideways at Nova. "Be who or whatever you like, as long as it's not a bobo."

"What's a bobo?"

"Bourgeois bohemian. Worse than a yuppie because they don't know their place. They wait for the artists to move into an area and then follow, gradually force them out."

"Like Greenwich Village?"

"And SoHo. Here, it was Yorkville, then Queen Street, now Parkdale. Christ, five years ago they wouldn't set foot in Parkdale unless it was to score a little blow. Now they'll likely close down the 'asylum' to make room for them, get rid of the annoying people who talk to themselves and ask strangers for cigarettes. Anyhow, the Market's next. I can barely afford to live here anymore."

"So if all these people are trying to be bohemian, why hasn't it spread? This so-called tolerance of yours."

"Because they don't really want to *be* bohemian, just have the aura of it, buy it and wear it. If the middle class ever disappears — the least tolerant group ever to materialize on earth — intolerance might give way to a little perspective. All of a sudden, people who thought a nice comfortable existence was what life was all about will be on welfare. It's happening now: well-educated welfare cases. As soon as they get over their initial shame, once they realize they're not alone, that it's not their fault, they might see there's more to life. If they don't, they'll commit mass suicide. Lemmings jumping over the cliff. But in reality it'll be like that Wild Kingdom scam."

"What Wild Kingdom scam?"

"Did you watch that show when you were a kid?" Nova nodded. "Well, they took it off the air because of the lemmings. Marlin Perkins and his crew drove a whole leap of lemmings over a cliff for footage. It wasn't a natural act at all, but they passed it off as one."

"That's horrible."

"Mmm. So these educated welfare types will go running off the cliff, prodded along by pressure and expectations instead of Marlin Perkins. Those who watch will think it's an entirely natural thing for them to do. The rich are very tolerant, they can afford to be. Not the middle class. Poverty's too close, so they only want to move up, get away in a pack, and seize power. Fitting in's the only way to do it, deviants need not apply."

Mrs. Philippa Maria Donahue knew all about fitting in, but didn't believe the middle class was likely to disappear any time soon.

"There must be other ways to increase tolerance," she suggested, but he shook his head emphatically. Nova pushed on. "What do you know about trying to fit in anyway?"

"I was supposed to be a big hockey star. My father's cliché dream. I was just about there when I discovered beer and girls. He tried everything to bring me in line but nothing worked, and it got to be that he couldn't stand the sight of me, wouldn't even look at me. So I left. Came down here and never went back. I haven't spoken to him since."

He climbed nimbly through the window, leaving Nova to ponder this new side of him. She had thought he was simply arrogant, the way she had thought all artistic types were, but his attitude made a little more sense to her now.

"How old were you?" she asked when he came back, the two remaining cans from the six-pack dangling from their plastic packaging.

"Sixteen."

"Was it rough?"

"Not really. I was pseudo-adopted by a great old bird. She taught me how to draw and encouraged me to finish high school over at Central Tech, pushed my stubborn ass into art college."

"It's kind of romantic."

"Romance has nothing to do with it. That perception's part of the problem, why people like you come down here to get fucked by a crazy artist or musician or . . . don't interrupt. People around here are family, better than family, actually, because you choose them and they don't judge or act all disappointed in you. I mean, I sent my parents an invitation to my first show, thought it might give them an opportunity to get over it. The assholes wouldn't even come to their son's show, but the whole fucking Market showed up."

"I'm sorry."

"Not your fault, is it," he said with a shrug.

"No, but you make me feel like it is." She stared at him, suddenly exhausted but angry. "I didn't come here with any agenda, you know. I didn't come here to get fucked by you or anyone else. So I played it safe, went with the pack, took the well-trodden path. Whatever." She punctuated the air with a chopping hand movement. "You have no idea why I'm here." Nova exhaled, finished her old beer, and looked away down the street so he wouldn't notice her eyes filling up.

Tommy smiled, sincerely for the first time. "Thatta girl, show us what you're made of."

She wiped her eyes with the back of her hand and took a deep breath. Tommy handed her a fresh beer and made a goofy kind of face. "Well, like they say in the country, the road less travelled sure gotta lotta stones."

Nova grinned a little and said, wistfully, "Maybe that will change one day. Maybe the natural order of things will collapse on its own somehow."

"There's nothing natural about order. It's an illusion."

"You know what I mean."

"No. I don't. As soon as people are inconvenienced, order

goes out the window. Inconvenienced, not even endangered. It's a myth. We're trained to believe in it so we obey. That's all."

"But it's necessary. If there was no order, there'd be riots every day."

"Bullshit. Have you ever been in an extremely long queue? For a bus, say. And folks begin to think maybe they won't get on. It gets later and later, it's the last bus of the day, and you just know there's other people down the line waiting, that by the time it arrives it'll likely be full anyway. Watch your order then. Elbows. If they had knives they'd stick you, right here."

Tommy grabbed Nova roughly around the neck and pretended to stab her in the gut. Although it was simulated, the very action made her uneasy. Nova wanted to believe that no one in her universe would stab another person for a seat on a bus, and said as much.

"There are some as would," he said.

"Well, I don't know any."

"See? There you go again. You don't have to *know* them, girlie-girl. Didn't you say you were American? Don't you know what people are capable of? Why kids are blowing away their classmates? Don't you read the history books? The newspapers? Do you think at all about what is happening around you?"

"Of course I do."

"So prepare yourself. This *is* Canada, but around here, it may as well be East L.A. Someone pulled a knife on a clerk in the shoe store the other day. The fucking shoe store! Some chick working in a Fast-Mart drew a fourteen-inch one on a thief. Last winter there was a stupid snowstorm and the transit was all messed up, and someone pushed a goddamn blind woman out of the way to get on the subway. I tell you. When a crisis comes, it's best to be ready for the worst. And I'm only talking about now. I'm not even talking about the day when all the yuppie spawn grow up twice as self-centred and materialistic as their parents. Christ, that's going to be a treat. They're not even going to know how to interact with the real world because they spend all their time with TV and cyberfriends. They'll be just kicking the poor people on the street, walking right over them, and thinking it's okay because their reality doesn't include such things."

Nova exhaled to release the vague tension of memory. She preferred to believe in common sense as a force to shield her, as though thought were one of the five — the true sixth sense — as though thought was common.

"Let's not talk about it, okay? I'll think about it. Let's go somewhere."

"I have no coin."

"I do. My treat."

"I don't like to take money from women," he said, though Nova knew it wasn't true. He rummaged around in a stack of papers and boards and withdrew a watercolour of a Kensington stall. The vegetables were all phallic and vagic, and a man in profile appeared relaxed and dreamy, sated by the sensuality of his produce.

"I'll trade you. You can have this for ten bucks, put it up on your wall for now, and then take it home with you when you realize you've had enough reality for this lifetime."

Nova thought she was getting the better end of the deal and offered twenty, which he accepted.

"I usually sell them for that anyway, but I was trying to show a little friendship. Thanks."

They headed off in the direction of her room so Nova could drop off her first piece of real artwork. Tommy Gunn had perfected the Market amble, an urban grazing pace, thick and gooey like condensed milk out of a can. Any faster and he might miss an opportunity to line up a couple hours of work, a free snack, the daily news of arrests and fights and affairs and breakups.

He stopped in front of the Patty King to consider a steaming pile of horseshit, suggested it was a deliberate act of the rider, indicative of what the men in blue really thought of the area they were meant to serve and protect.

"People all over town are screaming about the amount of human feces in the parks, but don't expect the mounted police to stoop and scoop."

From the look of the shit, the horse was definitely unwell. They followed the fly-covered puddles back to Vegetable Avenue, then north, Tommy all the while ranting and shaking his head at the obvious public health risk.

As they approached the cop, Tommy focused his energy on the beast. He could either calm or distress animals, depending on the energy directed at them. The horse stepped backwards and its rider tried to soothe him.

"Your horse needs new shoes, man," he said. "Look at his hoofs, all cracked like that. He's in pain."

Tommy bent down for a better look, stroked the foreleg nicely, but the horse reared up at the touch, surprising the rider.

"Get away, would you," the officer snarled.

"I thought these guys were trained to be docile." Tommy stood and moved away, curled his lip, stared into the horse's brown eyes and whinnied convincingly.

The horse bolted, secured himself retirement from the street.

"Now that's a musical sight," he said to Nova.

She looked around nervously and asked if he wasn't afraid.

"Of what? It's illegal to impersonate a police officer, but last time I checked you can still imitate a horse."

◆

After she secured her painting in her room, they strolled down to the Temp so Tommy could check out his mural in the light of day and ask the owner one more time if he wanted it touched up for a hundred bucks. He didn't, but he bought its creator a beer nonetheless. Tommy pleaded with the man to take the rest of the shitty art off the walls, to repaint, and eliminate the two-tone orange.

"I mean, I know what your decorator was trying to do, to pull the colour out from the sign in the back, but it stands alone. That's its effect and you've ruined it. The rest of the walls should be the same dirty white as the sky or the grey of the buildings. The colour is supposed to seem like an accident."

"Too depressing. We need colour in here."

They joined a table out front and Tommy cursed the tightness of the owner, ranted a little about poor taste, about being ripped off in the first place, and the possibility of sabotage.

"Did you hear about Whittaker?" asked one of the guys at the table.

"What?"

"Dead."

"What the fuck are you talking about, dead? I saw him yesterday."

"OD."

"Who told you that?"

"Buddy, down at the Bull."

Tommy finished his beer and got up. "You better not be spreading one of your rumours."

"Go and see for yourself. There's a wake planned for four o'clock over at the Plate."

Nova stood tentatively, uncertain how to proceed. She was surprised at the level of grief evident in Tommy's pale face, transforming it like a mask, only real. She hadn't expected he'd be capable of such concern for anyone other than himself, and for the second time that day felt there might be more depth to him than he let on. Rather than express a banal attempt at comfort, she simply hurried along beside him, glanced over occasionally, and waited for him to speak.

Keith Whittaker arrived early to ensure a good seat. He was curious, hopeful of packing the house like he and the Demics used to at the Blue Boot in London twenty-odd years ago. It was a macabre dream come true, the opportunity to be present at your own wake. He grinned as he imagined the looks on people's ugly mugs when they saw him sitting there and considered spying from inside — better yet, from the adjacent park — to get a full sense of the sadness exhibited, or not, depending.

The rumour had started at the Black Bull on Queen Street, and he hadn't even been there in a year. OD. Keith Whittaker, know him? Yeah man, OD'd. Everyone was ODing this summer, so it wasn't a surprise, only that Keith never touched the stuff, and what gobshite believed it could be possible? They phoned his house with condolences for his girlfriend and said there would be a wake that afternoon, it being sunny and Sunday and wasted days so much better with a purpose.

Positioned on top of the jungle gym, he watched with morbid prescience as one after the other, friends, enemies, acquaintances, arrived and hugged or shrugged. Keith was surprised to see some friends from way back in the seventies, and was touched to the point of tears. When a sufficient crowd had gathered, he sauntered across the street, feigning oblivion.

Only when the initial confusion ended did he tell them, "Ya bunch o' fucking goofs. You know I don't do that shit."

Tommy alternated between hugging Keith and punching him on the arm, uncertain of whether to be angry or happy, settling on both. After the third punch, Keith growled at him to "fuck off, would ya." He shook a little from the surreal, and a strange energy hovered around the patio like a fog of emotion. The grief people carried to disseminate in this spot had mixed with cautious relief, and since the owner had sent out several free pitchers of beer, many people became twisted and barely able to stand, the entire event bordering on disaster.

Nova stood alone in the farthest corner and thought of her own death, of the number of mourners likely to show up on her behalf. This fellow, whom she'd expect to die alone in the world by the look of him, commanded a steady stream of people to his wake, and she'd be hard-pressed to attract more than a dozen.

She wasn't certain if Tommy was loaded, or high, or experiencing a form of emotional insanity. He was steady on his feet, but his eyes shone with the wrong kind of light.

"Come," he said after about a half-hour of ignoring her. "I want to show you something." Tommy took her hand with an unexpected gentleness. It felt strange to walk up a street holding a hand, such an intimate and sensuous act, sometimes more so than a fervid sexual encounter. Now she really felt she was cheating on her husband, whose sweaty hand she hadn't liked to hold since the first year of their marriage.

They stopped at a corner vegetable stand and Tommy considered the potted garden plants displayed off to one side. He picked up a jalapeño pepper plant, and continued walking.

"Aren't you going to pay for that?" asked Nova.

"What for? It's nature. Nature shouldn't be for sale."

Nova thought Tommy could likely justify anything he put his mind to, and while she could see the logic behind his belief, theft was still theft and who was he to think the rules didn't apply to him?

They entered a pathetic parkette, no bigger than a medium-sized housing lot, barren but for two concrete tables and stools and a climbing contraption intended to resemble a dinosaur. They had to walk behind a row of bushes set at the back in order to reach the object of the visit.

"The martyr garden," said Tommy. "Martyrs of the edge."

Blood-red opium poppies dominated, and Tommy was so awed by the coincidence that he nearly convinced Nova of its significance, its parabolic nature: a garden that lives out the representations it was designed to honour. He explained how he had sown the first seeds ten years earlier, in a scheme to harvest the first Kensington Market strain of marijuana. When his first death occurred, he had been on the way to check on the initial buds.

"I didn't know the person too well, but it was the first time the grim reaper had even come close to me. Imagine that. Twenty-five years old and never touched by death. My own suddenly seemed imminent, fleeting nature of life, etcetera, etcetera, and I felt compelled to create something that would live and endure, not just as a view, like art, but as contributing to the universe. So I came up with the idea to plant a flower every time someone in the Market died. I didn't know it would grow into such a colossal project. I've got a list of about fifty names somewhere and eventually I'll make a plaque."

"What did you plant that day?"

"It's a bit cheesy."

"It can't be, because it's part of something so wonderful."

Tommy looked at her to see if she was serious, if she really was getting it.

"A black pansy. Velvety and black as coal. Guy was gay. Died of AIDS."

There was a tight patch of them now, concentric and dense. Somehow they'd remained pure, unaffected by pollination as though bees were either homophobic or not attracted to colourless petals.

"See the sweetgrass? It should be dominating because it's the only plant indigenous to this region. But it's about half as tall as it should be. Whereas those bastards . . ."

He kicked at one of the poppies and its delicate tissue-paper petals scattered on the ground, leaving a barren pod filled with the potential to kill.

"Next we have narcissus, thriving. That was put in for a dancer friend of mine who killed himself before he grew ugly with age."

Tommy bent down and used a pocket knife to dig a hole for the pepper plant in front of the poppies.

"If this garden really is reflecting reality, perhaps this'll protect him, keep the ornery old bastard alive a little longer."

Nova gave him an awkward hug, but he pulled away quickly.

"I really only brought you to see it because I hoped you'd understand the sanctity, would think about it, and if it caused you to think — at least to alter your impression of me — it would have a positive effect on the universe."

"You think I can be altered because of this?"

"Course you can, unless your mind is completely closed, and if it were, you wouldn't be here. Look, this is the present. Your body is changing, rotting really, as you stand there. Every breath you take you're breathing in shit and germs, and who knows what molecule is going to finally say, 'Hey! Let's get her.' Every little experience or sight or thing you eat changes you."

"It's a bit much to comprehend, really."

"Bah! Once you get it, it'll free you, make you start thinking of the immediate rather than worrying about the past or future. There'll be no space left in your brain for those things and you'll suddenly be able to groove with your immediate surroundings. It's a trip, really."

"Can I plant something sometime?"

"What for?"

"To commemorate someone. Someone who died for me."

He considered whether to expand his shrine in this direction.

"Is it why you're here?"

"In part."

He agreed with a shrug and they walked, arm in arm, down Vegetable back to the Plate. Tommy knew nearly everyone there and made the rounds, introduced Nova this time, and finally settled in next to Keith. All eight of the people at the table of honour were in their late forties; however, none could be accused of being middle-aged.

"Where'd you find this bloke anyway?" said Keith to Nova.

"Be nice, Keith, or I'll rip your teeth out," Tommy replied. "What's left of them," he added softly, and quickly dodged the imaginary blow he pretended to expect.

"Suck me bleeding arse."

"I caught her wandering through the Gaza Strip the other night and rescued her."

"Rescued me?" said Nova. "That's such a lie."

Tommy shrugged.

"I heard the other day they're releasing *New York City* on CD." The speaker had orangey hair, and Nova marvelled at how a man pushing fifty could pull it off without looking the fool.

"Yeah," replied Keith. "Some compilation of classic Canadian punk rock."

"Any dough?"

"Not worth talking about. Maybe get meself a pint or two."

"You're a musician?" asked Nova.

"You are sitting with the famous Keith Whittaker of the Demics," said Tommy.

"Never heard of them." She shrugged, dismissive of minor Canadian musical fame.

"Don't worry about it, love," Keith said. "You were probably only a wee lass at the time."

"I'm thirty-one."

"In that case, suck me bleeding arse, bitchka."

They all laughed, except Nova, who was still not accustomed to such conversation and not eager to become so.

"Are you still a musician?"

"It's not the fucking flu."

"Well, are you in a band?"

"No."

"How come?"

"Gunn!" he hollered. "Will you please tell your friend here about asking questions."

He told her, "Don't ask questions."

Nova took several long pulls on her pint, thinking that maybe she really was a little girl, naive and unfunky once again. Keith caught her frown.

"Smile, love. I didn't mean anything."

A distinctly un-deerlike man named Bambi was trying to catch Tommy's eye without drawing Nova's attention. Tommy finally looked in his direction and nodded.

"She's cool," he said.

"I've got some perfect Washingtons," said Bambi. "You game for a couple?"

"What's my cut?" asked Tommy.

"Half."

"Let's go." He turned to Nova. "I've some biz to deal with. Be back in about an hour."

She felt awkward and abandoned. Without Tommy's sponsorship Nova was clearly an outsider, and the people at the table ignored her. So she ordered another pint and listened politely. Soon, the empty chairs were filled by a pair of musicians who were pleased to see a new face among the regulars.

"Hi. I'm Rick, this is Jake."

"Nova," she replied and shook their hands.

"Up for a little Sichuan, Keith?" asked Rick.

"I just about died, ya wanker. What do you think?"

Rick shrugged and opened a black and tattered case containing a handcrafted mandolin. He pulled out the instrument and began to caress and tune it, explaining to Nova that an instrument is just like a woman, requiring a precise touch to make it sing. Everyone groaned, and Rick winked at Nova. He released his hair from its elastic band, and she realized he was the singer from her first night in the Market. She disregarded his cheesy comment and the rule about not asking questions because she needed to know if he'd written that song, needed another voice-of-God experience right about now.

"Sure did," he lied. "You liked it?"

"It was fantastic. It's about me. When I heard you singing it the other night, I thought you were singing it for me."

"I was, baby, I was." He glanced at his buddies so they wouldn't ruin the game, the chance to impress or maybe even get laid.

"Let me buy you and your friend a pint. No, I'll buy a round. God knows how long before my money runs out. May as well make the best of it."

"All right," said Rick. "A plate of pints."

Nova was beginning to feel a little bit drunk again. Draught was like that, at the Plate, in the sun, in the heat, with the crazy energy going to everyone's head. When Rick set a tin whistle on the table, she felt brave enough to pick it up and asked if she could play along, thinking these men were about to play traditional wake music.

"You know how?"

"Of course I do," she said.

"Give me a G, Jake."

"I broke my G string, buddy. God I hate that, always breakin' G strings."

Nova was the only person at the table to laugh, to have never heard the joke. Rick and Jake appreciated her attentiveness, the fresh addition to a somewhat cynical group.

"What'll it be, folks?" asked Rick.

A grey-haired woman with skin that nearly matched shouted out, "'Margaritaville.'"

"No!" snarled Keith. "It's my fuckin' wake, and I don't want that shite." Nova didn't exactly warm to this person who so obviously thought he owned the patio, perhaps the universe, as a result of a rumour of his death.

"We have dissension in the crowd, Jake. Your call."

"'Son of a Son of a Sailor.'"

A few of the people near the table shouted out bits of the chorus. Others shouted bits of abuse. Nova struggled with the whistle because it wasn't at all the type of music she'd anticipated, but it was fun to try, and no one really seemed to care when she stumbled or sat silent trying to get the hang of the tune. Eventually, they did perform "Margaritaville," and while some people groaned in protest, more enjoyed the chance to sing the words "It's my own damn fault." Rick and Jake allowed her to do a little solo and a few people even applauded her afterwards. Nova pleaded with them to run through the song a second time, told them she absolutely had to hear the part about living on sponge cake again.

"One more time, for the newcomer!" said Rick, happy to oblige a pretty young thing.

Their Jimmy Buffett repertoire, sung without the irony one might otherwise expect to find on an urban Toronto patio, augmented the surreal quality of the premature wake. Nova wondered why spontaneous music-making wasn't the norm in white-bread North America, like in Ireland, where a good part of the pub's essence is the enjoyment of music, day or night. The music had made her gran's wake bearable, and some relative or another had given her a tin whistle that she'd played everywhere. Even her ma and da had sung the songs, and they never sang at home in Cincinnati.

After the encore performance for Nova's benefit, Rick swallowed half his pint in one go, wiped the foam from his soup-strainer moustache. She was a bit disgusted when she thought about whether it ever got shampooed. All the guys at the table had some form of facial hair, thick mutton chops or little *bar-biches* or forked devil beards. She commented, phrased a statement of observation rather than a question, and they told her they were participating in a hirsute competition, growing the wildest style to see if it would be latched onto by the ovine young folk, the way the goatee had been by anyone under twenty-five who wanted to register as a hipster. The winner would collect a drink from each participant.

"And what if no one picks up on the style?"

"Their loss, really."

"Yours is a little grotesque," she said to Rick, oblivious to her rudeness now that she was fully tipped.

"Gee, thanks. I'll shave it off if you come see me tonight. I'm playing at the Greeks."

"I may do that. I never get to hear live music. I'll see what my friend's up to."

"Who's that?"

"Tommy. Know him?"

"Gunn? Yeah, I know him. He's your old man?"

"Good God, no. I just met him two days ago. He's showing me around is all. If he doesn't want to go, I'll come on my own. Just tell me where it is."

"Next street up, a few doors in. You can't miss it."

"With the little patio, and jazz?"

"Yeah. And the stench. Most people know it by its smell."

Tommy and Bambi returned in an uplifted state from a successful secret mission.

"I brought you a little present, a peace offering." He

handed her a small vial of oily liquid. Nova removed the little stopper and sniffed. It was very green and earthy, a familiar but unidentifiable scent. She dabbed a little on her index finger and smeared it across her neck and wrists. Tommy watched, smirking as she held her freshly perfumed wrist to her nose.

"Thank you," she said.

"You're welcome," he replied. "But it's for your hair actually, to stop the frizziness and bring out the curl, make you pre-Raphaelite rather than the porn star you find so offensive."

"But it's oil. I can't put oil in my hair."

"Sure you can. It's rosemary oil, totally natural. Here, give it to me."

He rubbed a little between his palms to heat it up to a thinner consistency and worked it into the ends of her hair and scalp. Perfect ringlets formed around her face and ears, and he adjusted a couple of stubborn strands with a coiling technique around his finger.

"Much better. Now, I think we need to initiate you, girlie-girl. Whatcha say?"

Nova looked around for a clue as to what this might mean.

"Don't be ascared. Have you ever committed a crime?"

Nova wondered about this.

"Not really," she replied.

"Not even lifting something from a store?"

She shook her head.

"Well, well, well. In order for you to be accepted into the pack, we'll have to do something about that. So we can trust you, know you're not a cop or nothing."

"What?"

"Something I've been wanting to do for a while now. You

can help me. It's not a real crime, more like a caper. We'll call it the great graffiti caper."

"You want me to paint graffiti?"

"Not exactly. I'll come by and get you under appropriate cover of darkness at three o'clock."

May 26

The pills help immediately. They really do. They help me think of Brendan as the type of husband women dream of, and he is: classically handsome, successful, responsible, symmetrical. I should consider myself fortunate. If I'm patient, if I learn and pay attention, he might become a little more passionate, or that strange and momentary need for passion will recess back to wherever it lay dormant. In the big picture of what's important in life, where does passion really sit? Isn't it an immature notion, as unrealistic as leaping out of bed to hurry to satisfying work? Maslow would have put it on his hierarchy if it were truly a universal need.

Routine and order have always seemed to help too, as though they are essential tools for maintaining an even mind. So, in the morning, I get up before he does to make his coffee, set the table for a simple breakfast. We share the newspaper quietly. Quick kiss on the cheek as he goes out the door. He doesn't speak much in the morning, so I don't speak to him. I wait until he gets home from a hard day at the office. I won't dress in an overtly sexy way, so it's not in his face all the time, but will try little things like lingerie as a reminder to him. Every now and then, I'll tart myself up and see if he's more comfortable with that.

Afternoons prove to be the only tricky part of the day, why, I suppose, they're filled with talk shows and soaps. Dead time. Without them, housewives might stream out onto the streets and protest their boredom.

◆

"Why don't we have a dinner party?"

"What for?"

"So I can get to know a few people better, have some laughs."

Brendan looks around the condo as though imagining what it might be like with couples placed nicely, like Royal Doulton figurines.

"Okay."

"When should we have it?"

"Saturday?"

"Who shall we invite? Brook and Ashley, of course. And you seemed to like Anton and what's her name."

"Jemmy."

"Right. What's that short for anyway?"

"Haven't a clue."

◆

There's a magazine that's like a guidebook for achieving a perfect life, printed in the colours necessary for a harmonious environment — no peach, I notice. It guides its readers through perfect theme parties with quaint, if impractical, items such as candles in brown paper bags on windy autumn nights. Better are the suggestions for attractively organizing objects you never thought to organize, and recipes to tear out and stick in a box.

My theme is the beginning of summer; my secret, distance from the past and past actions. I'm really trying to put an end to my dissatisfaction, to wrap it up in cheesecloth and poach the hell out of it, which is what I'm doing with the salmon fillets. In Pernod. Every action is designed as either a burial or a resurrection, endings and beginnings. I've prepared sorbets from the first of the season's raspberries to cleanse our palates between courses. Cleanse the bad taste I've left in Brendan's mouth. The tastes in my own. Baby asparagus spears, I read, not in the perfect-life magazine, somewhere else, make a man's jizz taste yummy, if that's at all possible. Bread kneaded and risen and peppered with rosemary from the patio. Finally, fresh peaches glazed in a brown sugar brandy sauce, flambéed. My eyes. My sights.

Blender drinks, melon daiqs, the exact perfect-life colour. Mmmms and ahhhs as we swallow the harmony. Smoked mussels on mini-toasts, my secret communion, shared now with my husband. It's no longer my own secret. It's ours.

It's not until the port and cheese that I am even remotely aware of the conversation as words. It was merely background noise until now. I emerge from some unknown dimension and the voices seem suddenly loud and intrusive.

"But statistically, born in 1962, you are a boomer." It's Anton, and he seems to be picking a fight with Jemmy's sister, Julia, for some reason. I liked her the minute she walked through the door, apologizing for the gift of wilting carnations bought from the vendor outside the subway station.

"Jemmy's embarrassed, says it would have been better to arrive empty-handed. She actually tried to grab them from me and pitch them."

"They're lovely," I lied, and she laughed.

"They're horrid, but she wouldn't let me pick some from her neighbour's front garden."

"Whose statistics?" she's saying now. "Sometimes they lump us in with Generation X."

"So you think we're Gen X?"

"No. Neither term fits. The experience hasn't been the same. I'm talking from a totally demographical point of view, not just a date of birth. I'm not bitter about the lack of opportunity, but aware of it nonetheless."

"I think of myself as a boomer," says Brendan.

"I know it. I suppose that's why we're included, because there are a few people who think the marketing is aimed at them, but in fact we're the Undefined Generation, a few years' worth of people not numerous enough to form a critical mass to be targeted. Forgive me if it sounds insulting, but you're just an example of someone who bought into the hype."

"It's a matter of survival," he said, dismissing her.

She frowned. Wouldn't let it go.

"I bet you were driving a beemer right out of university, weren't you? Maybe even in high school, your dad's car. Because it was a sign that you were one of them. But I tell you, you're not, no matter how many of the trappings you've managed to acquire."

"So where is your line of demarcation?"

"The recession of the eighties. When the term yuppie was coined, it described those who had "made it." Anyone in their twenties who hadn't at that point can't be defined as a boomer.

It was over. The well dried up and we were left struggling to squeeze into a place. We were working, just not going anywhere because there was no place left to go. No room at the inn, so be content to sit where you are. Gen X didn't even get a foot in the door. We did. That's the difference."

"And how do you explain that I was able to make it? I've risen to the top."

"You lucked out. You chose a career they didn't. They went into business and law. You went into computers when it was still a profession rather than a trade."

Uh-oh. Big point for Julia.

"I think you are bitter," Brendan tells her. "You're looking for excuses for your failures."

It's time to jump in here and advert a little disaster.

"Let's go out on the patio for some fresh air. Who needs a drink?"

Julia follows me into the kitchen to help with the orders.

"I'm sorry to put a damper on the conversation. I just couldn't take the smugness any more. I had to shake things up a bit." She smiles wryly.

"Actually, I kind of enjoyed it."

"Jemmy'll never bring me out with her again."

"I'd never guess you're sisters."

This makes her laugh. "The greatest myth of all time is that siblings are similar. I'd say it's next to impossible, particularly for sisters. Always competing for attention and praise. The only way to get some is to be different from the other."

"What's Jemmy short for?"

"Jemima." She arches one eyebrow. "The poor thing didn't want to be associated with pancakes or dark skin. Quite frankly, I think it's a beautiful name. I use it when I want to remind her she's getting a bit uppity. Drives her absolutely insane."

"They're funny things, names. Mine is a little joke my ma decided to play on her husband to force him to put aside his grievances. He refuses to acknowledge I share a name with the prince of England, calls me Phillie or Maria."

"How did that make you feel?"

"Like a bit of a pawn, really."

She nods as she considers this. "It's quite funny, though."

"It would be if it weren't me. Why is Anton so antagonistic towards you, by the way?"

"Is he? We used to date. I ditched him." She shrugs. "He tries to make me think I lost out on something really special. It was a bad idea to come. I figured it would be, but they insisted."

"I'm glad you did. I don't know a soul in this city and need to meet a few."

"What, you're not one of them?"

"One of whom?"

"The Toronto mafia. They've known each other their entire lives. Jem thinks they'll accept her, but they won't. Not entirely." She raises her fresh beer bottle in my direction. "Good luck to you."

We join the party on the patio, and Jemmy's telling Brendan he and I could be mistaken for brother and sister, we look so alike.

"Is that a sign of some sort of incest fantasy?" asks Anton.

"Just narcissism," I tell him, before I can check myself.

Ashley laughs because she thinks it's true.

Julia makes the comparison to those sick women who dress up their little girls to look like miniature versions of themselves.

"I'll never do that to my daughter," says Jemmy, patting her belly.

"You're expecting?" I ask.

"God! Can't you tell? I'm huge!"

Julia frowns at her sister, and Ashley says she can't wait to be pregnant.

"Why?" I challenge.

"I don't think a woman is fully formed until she experiences that."

Brendan glances at me and smiles before dropping his bomb. "Could you convince my wife? She believes it will diminish her."

I pretend to have a headache and excuse myself so I won't make a scene.

Different parts of my body pain me in perfectly isolated points of hangover. The port is now a needle behind my eyes, the rum in the daiquiris is doing a cha-cha in my stomach, and the wine provides a throbbing beat at the temples. I wasn't even tipsy, so it doesn't seem fair that I have to suffer so. In addition to the pain is an aura of anxiety, like a shadow not yet cast to the perimeter. Three aspirins and two Prozacs are my chosen cure, followed by a long hot shower to try to bring some colour to my face.

I leave a little note for Brendan explaining my hangover and a need for grease and eggs before I die. I think he has to work today, and if I can stretch out my absence, I might miss him and any confrontation that might arise out of my rudeness last night. At least I can postpone it until his raised voice won't feel like a hatchet in my skull.

There's a restaurant designed to resemble a diner down Cumberland and I assume the menu will reflect the decor, in content if not in price. I order the greasiest breakfast available, coffee, and a large orange juice for potassium. There's a toddler behind me, screaming, while Mom and Dad read the Sunday *New York Times*.

"Would you mind?" I say, trying to sound polite. "Could you . . . try . . . to amuse him. It's the head, you see."

"Not our fault you're hung over, and certainly not *his*."

Somehow, too many parents believe the world should revolve around them and their offspring, assume we all want miniature replicas of ourselves to show off and brag about. A childless woman in her thirties begins to draw suspicion and carefully worded queries. I've seen it too many times. The edge of pity, the assumption of infertility or lesbianism enters the voice, and eyes shift downward, away from damaged goods. Choice, my ass.

"Actually, it's not a hangover," I tell them. "Brain tumour."

They look at me as though I'm a leper, and even the child shuts up, sensing an end to his playtime perhaps. I nod at him and say thank you. They gather up blankets and rattles and plush toys spread around his side of the booth, put some money on the table, and depart, only casting a second eyeball at me as they leave. I feel a bit guilty for the lie, and on a Sunday, but they've left their magazine and I grab it for the crossword, forget about it.

◆

At the subway station behind the bookstore, a blind man plays a tin whistle. He reminds me of the monuments people the world over never notice unless they're tourists, erect and still, moving only when someone rushes by too quickly and close.

A cane positioned in a plastic yogurt container of alms grounds him. I listen to some familiar mournful melody, stare at the crazy eyes until my own tear, until I feel he must be aware of it. Surely the blind develop extraordinarily sensitive detectors of presence.

What separates me from him? A sense. A single sense. Maybe an accident. A gene. What would I do? The only thing I'd be good for would be hooking. Johns might be titillated to give it to a blind whore. Totally anonymous sex. Would they make faces at me, feel compelled to surprise me? With a blow? I wouldn't be able to identify them, so would they be more inclined to be nasty, or less? What is human nature? Cruel, if my man here must keep his cane in his money pot, which is what he's doing. Not for balance. It's an anti-theft device.

The anxiety returns, twice as black. I must be a nutter to be thinking of hookers and telling people I have a brain tumour. I don't want to think about blindness and hookers and brain tumours.

When I get home, a scrap of paper on the counter provides a bit of reassurance that Brendan's not angry with me, an invitation to attend a Jays' game later in the afternoon.

◆

The box comes with its own waitress — "hostess," she says, as though that elevates her. The two men flirt in her presence, talk like randy schoolboys in her absence, so I'm not certain why I was invited. Brendan has chosen to ignore me in order to ingratiate himself to his boss, our host, unrelated to our hostess in so many ways, though old enough to be her father. I just know that by the end of the game he'll feel entitled to deliver his ribald remarks directly to her, and Brendan will simply smile and nod and chuckle. I'm feeling a bit foul still from the hangover and too little sleep last night, so I try to watch the small figures on the field — it might seem I am in fact at the game and not in a hideous sports bar with a couple of tired clichés. The Jumbotron screen is too large, always in my peripheral vision, so my eyes instinctively go to the better image. I watch the fans in the stands and envy them when a successful wave ripples around the stadium.

"Why didn't they put these private boxes down at the front so you can see?" I ask.

"More room up here, more boxes," I'm told. "Just watch the screen."

But I don't like the screen. It forces me to watch what it tells me to watch when I want to catch a fielder grabbing his bag, for a laugh, for reassurance that he's real and not an obscenely overpaid representation of an athlete.

"I think I prefer the old-style stadiums," I say. "But I suppose it's more practical up here to have one that's covered."

"At times," my host says slowly, tentatively.

Brendan's eyes urge me to stop the conversation now.

"It generally being so cold and all," I continue. Oh, the look on Brendan's face. Butter wouldn't melt in his mouth right now.

His boss begins to describe Toronto weather patterns before Brendan has the opportunity to suggest I was having him on. He's told me a gazillion times about how irritating Americans can be with their misconceptions about Canada. In fact, I've received several directives about what I can and cannot say.

"Can I smoke in here?" Another taboo I've been warned about.

"Only in the bar."

"Excuse me then."

They tried to make the bar lively with posters and fake pennants and photographs, but it doesn't escape the bleak concrete oppressiveness of the stadium. Although the roof is retracted, it doesn't lessen the feeling of being closed in, captive observers of rich little men playing with balls.

◆

After the game, we *do* go to a hideous sports bar near the stadium. There are ten television sets suspended from the ceiling so that no matter where a person sits, the sightlines are free and clear. The screens show a popular program of real-life police chases. When it first went on the air, Brendan was enthralled, amazed that there were so many to film on American highways, and he waited for a crash. He hoped to be able to call one in and claim the five-hundred-dollar fee, not for the money so much as for the opportunity to participate. I think about the poor sucker in the stolen Range Rover on the screen, about to be arrested and humiliated on national television. Likely illiterate, he will smile when it's revealed he's on camera, a silver lining to a couple of months in jail.

"So, tell me, Philippa, how do you like Toronto?" asks the boss.

I look around me, loathing it at that moment.

"It takes some getting used to."

"Do you think you could settle down here?"

Oh lordy. Here it comes. This is what it's all boiling down to, right here, right now.

"I'd be crazy not to want to."

There. That's not really a lie. I might very well be.

Brendan reaches out and clasps my hand, squeezes it. He hasn't known this was coming, and when I look at him, I know he'll be smiling because this is what he wants. I thought

I married a Canadian in love with America, but I didn't. He only used America to make himself more marketable up here.

"Because we think Brendan's partner material," he continued.

Hand squeeze again, and I have to look now. He's so proud of himself. He's full of pride and wants me to be as well. He needs it, I realize, more than sex, food, maybe even money. He needs me to look at him and see success and be in awe. I suddenly feel sorry for him. More than sorry, pity, and it's a horrible emotion to feel towards one's husband.

"But I like to make certain the wives are happy."

I remove my hand from Brendan's. It's sweaty, and his wet limp dead-fish grip revolts me. I show it too, by wiping it on my thigh.

"If you want to work," he continues, "we can help with the red tape and find you another place within the firm. I've already checked with the Cincinnati office and received a glowing reference."

Brendan smiles at me, something of a proud-parent smile for receiving an A on my report card.

"But, if you don't want to, if your priorities are home and family now, that's fine too. No pressure."

"Thanks," I say. "I guess Brendan and I have some decisions to make."

June 7

She watched him swagger down the street, heard him whistle while swinging his load: a pair of brooms stretched across his shoulders as a yoke, with two partial gallons of flat white exterior house paint dangling on either end. A backpack stuffed with rags, a well-used tray, and a bottle of red wine completed the beast-of-burden look. Tommy always had a look for whatever scene from his life was currently playing out. Since this was a dual role — honest labourer and petty delinquent — he wore a black toque for the caper aspect of the evening, a pair of industrial green coveralls for the other.

His lightheartedness felt misplaced on a street that spooked her. At that hour, the street seemed needy, like a despairing widower sitting alone in a darkened room, feeling the vast emptiness of his world, staring out the window for a sign of life. Vacant, it was not just dead, it was deathly, haunted by a million displaced auras and the restless spirits of bodies snatched away too quickly.

It reminded her of downtown America, the place to avoid after dark. Garbage composted in the gutters and good-sized rats feasted because cats were no longer allowed out to hunt if they had a home. Those found wandering were rounded up and put out of someone's idea of misery. Corrugated metal fronts, rusty and tagged, covered the previously vibrant shops and broadcast the existence of the type of hooligans partial to breaking unprotected windows for sport. Nova wondered what kind of person would break into a place to steal vegetables.

All in all, she believed it to be a poor scenario for a date, if you could call it that.

"Isn't it dangerous out here at this hour?" she whispered.

"Only if you don't believe in ghouls."

"And if I do?"

"You won't get caught surprised."

"Why ghouls?"

"That's what I call them — the junkies and crackheads and freaks — evil spirits embodied in men."

"When you were on crack, were you a ghoul too?"

"Where do you think I got the definition."

"And now?"

"The ghoul has moved on."

"So it's an occupying force?"

"Yeah. I'm really a nice guy."

She wondered about the veracity of this statement as they reached the top of Clothes and turned right on Fish. Tommy slipped the poles over his head and set his equipment down on the sidewalk in front of the Roti Hut. He produced the wine with a flourish and a "voilà," twisted its cap, took a long swig, and handed the bottle to Nova.

"Have some courage."

"Courage or insanity?"

"Same thing. Okay, so here's the caper. See the fake graffiti along this wall?"

Nova scanned the length of the building. Cartoon-like characters danced in stencilled uniformity across its facade for nearly a block.

"This building used to be a school. Part of a college, where, among other things, they taught immigrants English. They're turning it into lofts and that crap is supposed to impress potential buyers, make them think they'll be living on the edge here. Graffiti as a marketing device. It makes me wanna puke. Like Keith Haring. Haring commercialized graffiti, popularized it. We're going to get rid of it."

"Give them the banality they deserve?"

"You're not as dumb as I thought."

"Thanks."

"It's the beginning of the end. It's gentrification, and if they want gentrified, they shouldn't try to mask it with their idea of hip. It's false advertising. We really should be using beige paint because it's part of what I call 'the great beige,' this turning everything into bland sameness."

He filled the tray and dipped his broom. "We have to be fast. Watch me."

The broom cut a long swath of white across the red and green and blue, was swung down to the tray and back in an efficient production.

"You try."

Hers was a feckless swipe.

"More paint. More energy. Pretend, for a moment, that it's something you dislike."

Once she found her coordination for swinging a broom, she fell into a maniacal frenzy of effort, imagining it as her past, a hieroglyphic account of her attempt to slide through life with all the Brendans and Brooks and Ashleys of the world. She whacked paint on the heads to obliterate their happy faces. She outlined giant phalluses across the bodies before covering them over. About halfway through, she stopped for another chug from the wine bottle and saw that Tommy had stopped at his end and was watching her, grinning.

"Get to work," she said, laughing, pushing the hair away from her eyes and unconsciously smearing paint across her brow.

In less than an hour, the wall was de-graffitied and they crossed the street to survey their work. Tommy was satisfied, and he put a comradely arm around his accomplice. "Don't say a word to anyone."

She breathed rapidly from the exertion of speed-painting, and sweat stung her eyes and rolled down her cleavage. Philippa's adrenaline level had never reached this peak. She was about to say so, that it would never be surpassed, and had changed her forever in a cleansing sort of way, when Tommy pushed himself against her, smothered her face with his own, and backed her into the doorway.

His tongue was exactly as she'd imagined just days before, and she offered her own, pulled him close. A voice she identified as her own this time told her to invite him back to her room.

"Sorry 'bout that," he said, releasing her and looking around. Nova staggered a moment from the rapid drop in pressure. "Coppers," he continued. "Come on. We best skedaddle."

"You want to come to my place?" she said, still thinking the passion was authentically directed at her.

"I would, but I've got to be up in a couple hours. You can take the evidence, though."

She was about to protest, but he was off before she'd collected the right words and worked up enough spit in her suddenly dry mouth to speak them.

"See you tomorrow," he called out.

◆

The next day, Tommy bragged to everyone on the patio that they were the culprits, surmising pints would be the reward. The previous night's pact of secrecy was meant to prevent her from claiming the glory before he could get clived — affectionate local talk for pissed, and in his case without spending a dime — for his efforts towards neighbourhood preservation. That they had skirted the cops earned him bonus points, and his technique was applauded.

In an effort to save face, Nova pretended she hadn't enjoyed the kiss, and Tommy shared the free pint with her in a show of friendship that made her feel a little bit better about being rejected one more time.

He resumed her re-education as though he was the Seeing Eye dog trainer who used the perfect chaos of the Market as a school for young yellow labs.

"Do you notice anything odd about the buildings across the street?"

Nova looked at the ramshackle, ugly storefronts, said they were all a bit unattractive and out of place beside the Victorian semis further south.

"Fuck. LOOK, would you."

She gazed at the names, at the windows on top of the stores, the architectural style she could only describe as boxy.

"How many are for sale?" he asked. "How many are for lease?"

"So?"

"That's what you need to be seeing. The surface is one thing, but there's this rumbling trembling force of change beneath it all. Those buildings will be bought and torn down and replaced with something pretty for your sensitive eyeballs."

There didn't seem to be anything wrong with that. Nova thought the buildings could easily disappear, like the shit hawks, in the name of public service and health.

"Just the other day, I saw a couple of people walking down the street with some sort of plan in their hands. I asked them what it was but they scurried away from me, like it was some big secret treasure map I was going to steal. And you know what I think it was? I think it was a developer's plan for town-houses there."

"To go with the lofts."

"And then Starfucks and Pecker's and the SASMART will start to carry Calvin. All the hefty old women will have to march over to Eaton's to find big underpants, and there won't be a single housedress to be found for miles. The people who move in will all start to order their groceries over the Net, direct from the food terminal, and half the stores around here will close, the owners displaced once again. Finally, even if we wanted to sit here, with cellphones ringing every five seconds and loud voices shouting soap opera names at each other, there won't be a single chair to be found. It'll be all pseudo-bohemian actors and writers searching for their precious muse. We'll all be sent to the park, because the new folks won't tolerate an occasional scuffle, spilled beers, cigarette smoke outdoors."

Nova stared ahead and felt a bit queasy with guilt. Her dissociative state deepened in response to Tommy's rant, and Mrs. Philippa Maria Donahue was placed a little farther back on her shelf.

"Shouldn't you be practising your tolerance?" she asked. "Isn't change natural?"

"Sure, a little natural change is fine, but not massive redevelopment. Some people want everything neat and tidy, 'zif that can prevent the chaos from creeping into their lives. Others need everything chaotic so the occasional tidy times can feel like a vacation. Not too much, or else they get bored. I assume you got bored with tidy."

Nova nodded slowly, thinking peach, thinking of how she tried to force order on her life.

"I really don't give a fuck how others choose to live their lives, just as long as they quit trying to impose it on my own. I mean, they might even rename Kensington Avenue because some stupid assholes in Willowdale have a street named that too and could get confused about where they live or something. God forbid a taxi should drop them off down here at two in the morning."

"All right, enough already," she said.

Her participation in the "great graffiti caper of '99" did effect a degree of trust, though Nova had discovered by now that historical presence was the only guarantee of it. The Plate was like an old boys' club, so that even the obviously insane, obnoxious, rude, and intrusive were accepted if they'd been around long enough. People knew one another for ten, twenty years, and when they occasionally departed for the promises/drugs of Vancouver, jobs teaching English in Korea, prison, rehab, stabs out there in the real world, always upon their return, a family — perhaps dysfunctional, who's to judge, really — awaited with a bed, a meal, some work. Few still lived in the Market because of the new rents, but something sucked them in, brought them back — call it acceptance or tribal instinct or custom. Call it community, such an old-fashioned notion. But there was a rare and comforting sense of being among friends in a relatively unchanged place.

Nova's only enduring relationships were those dictated by blood and genes and she wondered if this had somehow stunted her development, too much of the same outlook influencing her own. She'd never developed lasting friendships because she was constantly shifting shape.

Soon, the animated conversation lifted Nova out of her self-reflection, and she listened to a tale about a Colombian prison. She knew this time not to ask questions and figured out on her own what the sentence was for. The man didn't fit her preconceptions of a criminal, as she'd never met one before, and she wondered if perhaps he was lying, bragging to prove how much tougher he was than the rest. He seemed too bright and educated to do something like that. She leaned towards Tommy and whispered her question, not wishing to offend.

"Speak up, lassie, I can hardly hear you above the smell of grilling sardines."

"Is he for real?"

"Remember what we talked about earlier. We've got a collection of Ph.D.s and M.A.s for company. That guy there quotes Chaucer while he hangs drywall, and that one's an architect who's tired of having his vision for a better world of buildings rejected. We're all just waiting for the switch."

Now the prison guy talked about karma and being part of the universe, and how the Market was a microcosm of that, how every person who entered affected it, brought in a new strain of cold virus and spread it by touching too many fruits for tenderness, caught it off a bag of rice from whatever country had produced a new strain that summer. Every thumbprint left molecules of skin and grease, caused a change, every aura affected another, and someone came up with the idea of a documentary to chart the effects.

They'd get a team of about five people with cameras, choose a tourist, follow him to his first stop, pick up the trail of the first person he speaks to, and so on. It'd be best if it began with someone displaying emotion that got passed around, to show how a little bit of anger or courtesy ricochets around the world and comes back at you. Maybe if karmic phenomena could be captured on film, people might finally get it. They'd win the Nobel Prize for both peace and science, share the profits, and take a collective trip to Oslo.

There were a few tales of instant karma and a segue from the sacredness of cows to how the levels of hormones consumed from their meat affects reproduction. Breast cancer, testicular cancer, early puberty, infertility. If we're going to alter our reproductive systems, why can't it be a positive evolutionary change? Why, for instance, shouldn't women grow a third tit instead of having to get one cut off? Nova suggested the best place for such genetic mutation to manifest itself was the middle of the forehead, so when a husband kissed his wife goodbye there, it would be more gratifying for them both.

The suggestion broke the remnants of awkwardness towards her, and Tommy elaborated on it, proposed it as something to hold onto at other times.

But if the human race was becoming infertile, that was the best evolutionary trick yet: greed-induced extinction of the species. Maybe the vegetarians would survive and they'd eventually get back on all fours to sniff around for nuts and berries and truffles.

"Ever seen a pig sniff out a truffle?" asked Tommy. "They use the females, and the truffles smell just like a male pig. That's why they go insane, why they bother to look for a mushroom."

Their laughter and boisterous conversation acted as a flare to attract others from duller company, and soon tables were pushed together to accommodate a larger group. Nova introduced herself and was greeted, with varying degrees of civility, by Collette, Jennifer, and Jed.

Three pints and the wide range of conversational subjects helped Nova relax enough to feel like a Market cat lounging in the sun, and once her defensiveness no longer seemed like judgment, people included her more in the talk. She turned her face to the sky and saw striations of cloud and early-evening shades of pink. It reminded her of a raspberry flaky pastry, and she was suddenly a little peckish.

"What do you call those sorts of clouds? Stratus? Nimbus? I can never keep them sorted in my head."

"It's a mackerel sky," said a gravelly voice down the way.

"But what's the scientific name?" asked Nova.

"Who needs science when there's such a perfect description," Tommy said. "Poetic. A mackerel sky." His mismatched eyes began to water in what she thought was an excessive display of emotion over a description, no matter how lovely it might be.

"Don't misinterpret, doll. I got this thing, this weirdness, called crocodile tear syndrome, for lack of one of your scientific terms, where I cry sometimes instead of salivate, and drool all over the place instead of crying. A kinda cross-wiring of the two glands. Thinking of a mackerel made me hungry."

The guy was cross-wired all over the place and Nova Philip saw the defects as refreshing idiosyncrasies. Brendan had been so tiresomely predictable, his words and deeds calculated to produce a minimum of variance.

"My God," she thought. "He probably subconsciously selected me so he could imagine he was fucking himself."

Nova offered up her theory for debate and sided with the position that extreme narcissism is a manifestation of arrogance, not insecurity.

"So if you really do look alike, what was *your* attraction to *him*?" said Jennifer quietly. Tommy hissed and Collette said "Meow." Nova smiled sheepishly at each of her defenders and confessed, "I guess I thought it validated me."

"Validation is for parking tickets," said Tommy.

"Yeah, right," challenged Collette. "And size doesn't matter."

"Not a worry of mine," he stated, receiving groans from the entire group. "What? You want proof?" He scraped his chair back from the table, and as he rose, began to unfetter his evidence.

"Save it for someone who cares," said Collette with more than just a little disgust. She turned to a giggling Nova and advised: "Don't encourage him."

Tommy stuck out his tongue and muttered that some

people have no sense of humour. Collette ignored him and began rummaging through a large knapsack beside her chair.

"I have something that would look great on you," she said to Nova, and pulled out a slinky acetone dress, deep purple in colour. As Collette held it up for appraisal, Jennifer's eyes were drawn like a magpie's to the shiny material. Nova caught the look of interest and saw that her black hair held the same tint as the dress.

"I think it would look better on her," she said, a little reluctantly, but thought it might be the proper protocol.

She handed off the garment and Jennifer immediately slipped it on, pulled off her stretch pants underneath to hoots and catcalls.

"How about this, then?" said Collette, handing over a lime-green and blue striped tube top. "They're so back in style this year."

"God! I haven't seen one of those things in years. Remember how the boys used to try to pull them down?" Nova thought it was quite a sassy little article and asked Collette how much.

"Five?" she suggested, expecting a barter. Nova pulled out her wallet and paid without question, took the top down to the toilet, and put it on. Of course when she went back upstairs, several of the men tried to pull it down, boys still being boys. Nova enjoyed the game because she felt she was back in the schoolyard, without adult cares, playing a variation of dress-up.

It was essential to continue to celebrate her initiation into this life, but she really required food before another pint, so went to the bank machine on Clothes Avenue. There was a little lineup and the machine seemed to choke on each request for cash. "Come on, baby, give daddy his dough," the man ahead of her crooned, and thanked the machine when it finally spat out a ten-dollar bill.

Her card was consumed and replaced with useless instructions to contact her branch. It wasn't surprising that Brendan had acted so quickly and vindictively, only that she hadn't predicted it and withdrawn enough cash to exist upon until she could begin to think about work.

She returned to the Plate and Tommy begged her a pint and a plate of crisp and greasy fish cakes. They latched onto a flush couple in need of a little diversion, and when the sun moved behind a street sign Tommy shimmied up the pole and bent the speed limit to a more accommodating angle. Another round was ordered to celebrate the last rays of sun as it set behind the SASMART. He winked at Nova and told her, "Don't worry. It's easy."

They spent the rest of the evening making up words, tried to settle on one to describe the feeling they shared over the sunset, a word available to other languages but not English. Nova suggested "sol-i-stice" and it was rolled off each tongue. That agreed to, they tried to create one for the smell of the humidity switching subtly from day to night, noticed there weren't enough words to describe smell.

Mrs. Philippa Maria Donahue awoke feeling quite ill from the beer, quite panicky that she'd stepped farther into the realm of Nova, an adulteress, possibly a slut. She searched her brain for a recollection of satisfaction, looked on the floor for evidence of proper precautions. Tommy lay snoring beside her, oozing a slightly acidic scent as he sweated out the alcohol, and she wanted him gone, without a morning cuddle or sleepy sex, out of sight and mind. It took a fairly rough shake from a standing position beside the bed, but she woke him awkwardly and they barely spoke as he dressed, which well suited her because she didn't know what to say, and more, didn't know what she wanted to hear. He was shy about it all, which suggested it was not a regular occurrence for him and made the absence of a condom wrapper less worrisome.

She had exactly enough change to get herself a cup of coffee, thought the boys at the Casa Açoreana would likely take pity on her and provide a refill, and they did. She tried to remain calm, tried to swallow her panic, as though it could nourish her. Truly penniless for the first time in her life, the only thing that prevented her from feeling squalid that morning was to view her situation as a choice with unavoidable consequences. It had been absurdly simple, thus far, to leave a marriage, and of course the process must include some degree of difficulty or else everyone would try it.

Other Market residents in apparently similar financial states stopped by for the free refills and chatted unashamedly about overdue rent. Collette arrived, beaming at Nova with a sly and mischievous glint in her eyes. She complained good-naturedly about needing three bucks for a pack of smokes and having nothing left to sell.

Nova glanced at her engagement ring, and with the promise of 10 percent commission, secured a deal with her to hawk it.

"Not on the street," she said. "You have to go to a proper place. It's worth a fair bit."

As she slipped off the ring for the first time in five years, she examined her hand, thought it was wholly diminished and quite ugly without the sparkling diamond.

"Don't sell it. Pawn it, and bring me the ticket in case I want to get it back."

"Get it back, or go back?" asked her broker.

"God! Am I really that transparent?"

"There's a bet on over at the Plate."

Nova felt a little sick.

"What kind of bet? Who's betting?"

"Tommy started it. How long you'll last."

Nova couldn't hide her hurt, so Collette tried to reassure her. "I've got a toonie riding that you've got more spunk than they're giving you credit for."

"What's Tommy saying?" she said, angry, humiliated, feeling duped.

"You actually care? Give it up, girl. Prove 'em wrong and win me the kitty. I'll share it with you."

◆

With the two hundred dollars from her ring, coupled with stubborn pride, she created a game of how little she could spend. "Five-Dollar Days," she named it, to make it seem less like life and more like living a sale at Wal-Mart. At one of the bakeries, a bag of several day-old loaves cost a dollar and something called Canadian Tire money was accepted at par. Most of the veg stores sold quarts of less-than-perfect fruit, practically gave it away, and she discovered that near-rotten produce is more flavourful than what she was accustomed to, the under-ripened, over-engineered fruits and vegetables designed to endure long-distance travel and still look pretty. She bought a tin of smoked mussels and wiped the oily tin clean with her hardened bread.

In her foraging for the cheapest possible sustenance, Nova discovered an entire range of food formerly ignored: grains and beans and other legumes. Lentils she'd tried once in an Indian take-away place, and here there were even different kinds and colours. She'd often comforted herself with baked beans on toast for lunch, but couldn't say for certain if they were really white or navy in their sauceless state. Her world of rice had been ruled by speedy Uncle Raj, that vaguely Indian character promoting a vaguely ricelike starch substance, nothing resembling the brown, long, short, basmati, thaimati, jasmine, black, or wild varieties.

She soon realized that the worst thing about her brand of poverty was not going to be hopelessness, but monotony, for without a kitchen, all these options were lost to her; without money for amusements, she'd be forced to nurse a half-pint at Kim's and content herself with watching people go by. In fact, the parade was more entertaining than any sitcom, and when she thought to imagine the world around her flickering on a little screen, she began to appreciate its value.

There was the woman with a wearable petting zoo: a pair of cockatiels perched in her candy-floss hair, occasionally hopping down to her shoulders. She squeezed a docile rabbit under one arm and held a kitten, more gently, in the crook of the other. Nova thought the woman resembled a combination of all three species, and wondered if the birds ever shat on her.

The rabbit, she was told, was beginning to act like the kitten and the latter was exhibiting some bunny-like tendencies. Nova asked for a demonstration, and sure enough, when placed on the ground the kitten made a few hops in her direction. And no, the birds never did.

Many kids in the neighbourhood had coloured hair as though from a Kool-Aid package, and Nova learned the powdered drink could indeed create a temporary rinse. When queried about the process, they told her that her hair wouldn't work, was too dark, but they'd bleach it out for her if she so desired. There was a particular shade of green Nova thought would suit her, would accentuate her eyes, so she added this to the list of self-improvements she'd make after she found work. She wasn't convinced green hair was a suitable colour for employment-seeking.

Straight-looking people shopped and seemed oblivious to the strangeness, which made her wonder if they were really straight, like she used to be, or fakers, fitting-inners. She still couldn't prevent herself from taking long assessing questioning looks.

Tommy Gunn had begun to treat her more gently, as though status deprivation earned her his acceptance, or the sex did. They never spoke of the sex, nor of his humiliating wager, lost, since she hadn't fled immediately after their drunken entanglement. She refused to give him the satisfaction of seeing her upset; besides, there was already another bet on as to who would be the next to die, making the speculation surrounding her seem petty and insignificant. And Nova had larger concerns: she needed introductions and work and the small kindnesses of strangers.

In fact, she used Tommy to meet dozens of people, and it seemed everyone she encountered had earned some sort of affectionate, universally known nickname: Eric the Thief, Holy Joe, Tricky, the Fighting Austins. Nova wanted to earn one also, not just attach it to herself. She'd even accept Porn-Star Girl if it was meant affectionately.

Tommy also prepared a little exercise for her, sent her off with a list of cryptic clues to test, to train, her eyesight.

"Dyslexic medicine. An unreadable book. Food opportunities. Fish out of freshwater." One by one she picked them off, the backward N at the Chinese herbalist, a book-shaped artifact bolted to a post. Pizzabilities. The fish she never found, and he led her by the hand and took her to the sewer grates marked with simple yellow icons.

"Three out of four. Not bad, girlie-girl."

She systematically began a job search at the foot of Kensington and asked every store, restaurant, and bar if they wanted cheap, under-the-table labour. Some places were wary of illegal activity, having black marks on their records for misdemeanours involving blind eyes, contraband cigarettes, drugs, and closing times.

Meat Mayhem, however, desperately needed employees after a recent exodus of staff to month-long vacations in various European motherlands. Nova told them she had an uncle who was a butcher, and that qualified her to stand behind the counter to select and weigh and slice and wrap. They dressed her in orange polyester that caused her to sweat and instructed her in the operation of the slicer and the scales: always give the customer a little more than requested. It was too busy in the store for customers to complain, and even if they did, their voices were seldom heard above the din of the number caller and shouts for chicken breasts and salami. After standing in line for a half-hour, people only wanted to grab their meat and get out. Nova was elevated from the customers and, halfway through her first Saturday shift, stood mesmerized by the mass of people pushing towards the front, cursing and crushing one another. She watched as a grinning man reached out his hand and systematically squeezed the ample breast of the woman beside him. The woman didn't make much of a fuss. She shouted something Nova couldn't hear, and whacked him. He just stood there grinning like a simpleton, which, she supposed, he was, and she kept her eye on him in the event he turned out to be a serial squeezer.

She didn't have a whole lot of opportunity for such sightings. Meat Mayhem served two thousand customers that single day, sold nearly ten thousand pounds of ribs and breasts and thighs and shanks, so Nova mostly thought of knives, food shortages, and starving children. She felt as though she'd been put through the grinder herself.

On a fifteen-minute break, she joined the butchers out front for a cigarette.

"You're not allowed to smoke here," they told her.

"Why not? You are."

"It looks bad to the customers. You look dirty. The girls are all clean, fresh girls. If you want to smoke, you have to go in the back."

The men were all white-coated, like doctors, but their uniforms were bloodstained. Nova wanted to crush their superior air and considered telling them they were fooling no one, that their trainers and baseball caps further distinguished them from the medical profession.

The back stank, layers of stench, ferrous and carnal and scatological. Flies swarmed. Wasps. Black garbage bags leaked rivulets of blood where still more insects clotted in their chosen ambrosia.

"Fuck this," she said, because really, such conditions were too odiferous, no matter how tolerant she was meant to be, how familiar they were supposed to become, and she ground out her cigarette in a wasteful action, leaving a trace of nicotine in the mix.

Five hot and airless, carcass-filled hours later, hours spent helping the butchers dump buckets of bloody dead animal parts into the display cases, Nova developed a new inclination towards vegetarianism. It wasn't really a matter of eco-narco-feminist leanings — she had no politics around meat apart from the new and vague unease about the possibility of hormonally produced third tits. Her new aversion had more to do with the sight and smell of meat losing its appeal, the way donuts had after a week's work at Krispy Kreme. Fifteen years later, she still couldn't choke one down.

◆

The heat had begun to affect her; its relentless oppressive weight bore down and prevented her from summoning enough energy to complete the simplest tasks of shopping or cleaning. It was forty-five degrees under the roof of her room and her windows were not placed with the intention of catching the cooling southwesterly winds off the lake. Who could have known seventy-five years ago that access to the breeze would become so essential? These houses were constructed to outwit snow and cold, not heat and humidity. Mrs. Philippa Maria Donahue had never experienced weather as such a formidable and constant adversary and was ill equipped for the challenge.

After work, crabby and unconvinced that this was her best employment option, thinking herself deserving of a reward, just the once, she thought she'd violate her boundaries. The swimming pool was only across the street, not a true decampment. She blew five bucks on a fifties bikini, hoped the previous owner had no nasty infections. Philippa Maria Donahue had never been in a public pool, and she tried not to think about foot fungus lurking in the cracks of the tiles, the possibility of lice and scabies and children's piss. It made her feel diminished to be in one now, vulnerable, violated by the disease of limited options, but the water was cool and if she kept her eyes shut she could pretend she was back at the lake. But the vision of the lake summoned the voice of Brendan, telling her she was too fat for her bikini, and next thing she knew, she was breaststroking her way down the length of the pool.

On her second day of work, Nova decided to pick up her spirits on her lunch break in Tom's Place. It was a well air-conditioned store, and the voluminous disarray of clothing provided a perfect excuse to spend a good deal of time searching for sizes and proper matches among racks of designer samples. When Nova stepped out of the changing booth, adorned from head to toe in Ellen Tracy, Mrs. Philippa Maria Donahue appeared in the mirror and startled her. She wasn't gone at all, and Nova Philip didn't look incongruous. She looked tired and in need of a little bit of makeup, but her core being had clearly come out of hiding to tempt her back to respectability.

That evening, Tommy dropped into Meat Mayhem to see how she was faring.

"Not well," she said. "Can you buy me a drink?"

She was irritable, thinking she might be a fool. She missed her air-conditioned peach condo, her closet full of clothes. She thought she lacked the stamina necessary for this type of life. Sipping a beer at the Plate, she bemoaned everything: the heat, the piggish customers and their meat, the butchers and their superiority. She noticed he wasn't affected by the heat and asked rather snidely if it had anything to do with willpower.

"Willpower? Hardly. I'm so fucking dehydrated I can't afford to sweat, haven't even taken a leak all day. Whatever made you think I had willpower?"

"Never mind."

"It's gettin' to you, isn't it?" said Tommy. "You're thinking of going back."

"It's horrid work. I haven't had a decent meal since I arrived . . . and I look awful."

"What made you think it would be easy?"

Nova said nothing.

"There is no money tree," he continued. "Or else I would have found it years ago."

But before too long, a man named Jorgé joined them and offered Nova three hundred dollars for her hair. Most wigs came from straight hair, he told her, and long curly black locks were a premium. Nova thought of her tenuous mood, of the luxury of a new used frock, a hot meal. She thought she might be more comfortable without the covering of hair. Mostly, however, she thought about the full transformation a haircut might achieve.

"Will you give me a decent cut afterwards?"

"Of course."

"Will you dye it green?"

"Sure."

"Okay, when?"

"No time like the present."

She curled her lip at Tommy and taunted him. "I think I found the money tree."

◆

The hair salon was like a funhouse to Nova, a Romper Room for grown-up girls. While Jorgé closed blinds and turned on lights, put on a Leonard Cohen CD, Nova wandered around and touched things to make it all seem real: an ancient stand-up hair dryer, big jars of blue Barbisol with combs in them, an orange wig modelled by a chipped Elvis bust.

"When I was a girl, I wanted desperately to be a hair-dresser," she said, pumping the pedal of an antique barber's chair. "I had one of those doll's heads with hair that pulled out and little pink brushes and curlers and clips."

"And?" said Jorgé.

"My parents told me only trashy girls became hairdressers."

"Right. And only gay men too," he laughed. "My mother and father still don't quite believe I'm hetero."

Jorgé watched as Nova moved restlessly about the room. He understood how women could suddenly become skittish about losing an identifying aspect of their appearance and lit a joint to relax his customer.

"Don't worry," he said, while holding the smoke in his lungs. "I do my best work a little stoned. I'm more meticulous, less impatient."

He passed the joint and sat her in a chair, turned it away from the mirror to prevent her from fleeing as the first handful came off. He carefully placed the hair lengthwise in a florist's box, chatted with Nova about her husband, expressed compassion and understanding, and promised to make her look like a new woman.

"Really," he said. "Long hair is so passé. I'm sick to death of the retro-hippie thing, much prefer moving forward. We should all move forward, like you're doing, take a few risks in life. Nothing like a new hairstyle to do it for you too."

Nova chatted endlessly, thanks to the dope, about the Market and the freedom she felt, the restrictions too. She asked him why there couldn't be a balance, and he told her there could, but she couldn't expect to just get up out of the lap of luxury and immediately find it in a little slumming. That shut her up and she listened to a song about being sentenced to twenty years of boredom, fell into a reverie close to sleep.

When Jorgé finished, nearly two hours later, no trace remained of Mrs. Philippa Maria Donahue. The woman in the mirror looked ten years younger, but ten years wiser. The green tint on her black hair had a velvet-like sheen, and since she'd braced herself for a more shocking transformation into a Kool-Aid kid, the colour didn't transfix her as much as the cut. A boyish girl stared back.

"I could walk right up to my husband, and there's not a chance in hell he'd recognize me. I barely recognize me. I could pick him up in a bar and he wouldn't even know it was a trick."

"It suits you. Look how the green makes your eyes pop right out of your head. You have excellent bone structure in your face that was hidden by the long hair."

"I love it," she said. "Thank you, thank you, thank you." Nova turned her head this way and that, tousled the curls a bit, tried to adjust. "Do you think they'll fire me from Meat Mayhem?"

"Probably."

Nova thought of this as she admired herself, and Jorgé started tidying up.

"Here, let me do it," she said. "It's the least I can do."

Jorgé handed off the broom and rolled another joint while Nova swept.

"You want a job doing that?" he asked. "We could use someone."

"Are you serious?" she said.

"I couldn't pay much."

"It doesn't matter as long as I can eat and pay my fifty-buck-a-week rent. Can I shampoo?"

This caused Jorgé to laugh. Of course she could shampoo, he hated that intimate part of the job. He told her he'd check with the other stylist, but since they'd been extremely busy now that wild cuts and colours had crept into the mainstream, he didn't think she'd object.

"Come by tomorrow, after noon, to confirm."

◆

The next morning, Nova went to Clothes Avenue for a look among the racks of Easter-coloured prom dresses, paisley shifts, and halter dresses. Somehow, the shape of women's bodies had changed over the decades, and her newly enlarged breasts and wider hips were apparently more fifties than sixties. The young woman behind the counter admitted to having a rare twenties shape and was out of luck since she didn't want to pay for alterations. Alterations would take the fun out of a twenty-dollar dress.

Nova admired herself in a perfectly new silk sleeveless dress with matching overcoat. Very Jackie O, she thought, but Jackie O was a past ideal. Nova Philip must discard such ideals.

She tried on the next dress, a paisley haltered Marilyn thing. It seemed to be homemade, with some poor finishing, but all-in-all quite an accomplished bit of sewing. Nova knew about homemade, how her mother would sew on a label to appease her apprehension that someone would check. "Poor Ma," she thought. "She could never relax about having money."

"I'm going to wear it," announced Nova, passing the sales clerk ten dollars. She looked around at all the discarded clothing, thought there was no need to buy anything new ever again.

"Who buys the prom dresses?" she asked.

"Girls who never got invited. They're reclaimed, worn in an ironic sort of way."

Nova wandered around in her new look, reclaimed herself, but without the irony, went to see Jorgé and got herself a trashy vocation.

Now that she felt authentically localized, tribalized, or synthesized, Nova Philip snapped to the grid of the Market more naturally. Once she stopped focusing on her chosen path, which boundaries to keep and which to ignore, both space and time seemed to expand. Her imagination amused her now that it was allowed to roam freely, and she occasionally wondered if Kensington tap water contained hallucinogens.

Marketeers, as some self-referred, thinking themselves equal parts juvenile club members and gallant adventurers, strutted down the middle of the street waving as though in a private parade. Too many trundle buggies crowded their sidewalks, so they claimed the road for themselves and told aggrieved drivers to get a parking spot. It wasn't pedestrian rage — they never got aggressive — rather, a form of creative resistance. Nova made it a ritual to walk about each day with no purpose but to say hellos, found herself falling into the habit of using the road as a more efficient path, found herself feeling entitled to do so.

She learned of a locally produced sitcom from the seventies, called "King of Kensington," and met the current monarch, a gingery fellow with a stack of *Outreach* newspapers for sale.

He'd given himself the title when the program went off the air, even before booze had really affected his other prospects. Nova saw him every day, laughing and boasting and shouting his title, and she'd share whatever small change happened to be in her pocket.

It became apparent to her that Vegetable Avenue sliced the Market in half. The east-west divide was both geographically and socially significant, and Fish Street was a further demarcation for upper and lower. Though she lived and worked in the lower east side, she mostly drank in the west, and it was this that defined her. It was a microcosm of the entire city, composed of neighbourhoods indicative of lifestyle. She thought that if Spadina Avenue were a river, the west side would be its Left Bank. If Toronto were really a world-class city, the defining districts would have more inventive, appealing names, rather than the unimaginative Queen West and West Queen West; College Street; The Beach: nothing terribly evocative to create a proper mythology for their habitués.

Kensington, on the other hand, immediately evoked the image of a palace, then challenged perceptions with an impertinent affront to its British namesake. Not only was it filthy and decrepit and filled with non-white faces, this Kensington was loud, but in a singularly musical way, whether from the loudspeakers, the bands, the foreign languages spoken so much more sonorously than English, tony accent or not. She thought the Market's movement and activity should be marked on a page, as notes in a composition. Some days, her life was a full-scale opera. Fridays were scored with ambient and acid jazz, gearing up to funk as the day progressed. Saturdays could easily be translated through jungle and hip-hop, and Sundays a dulcet pop song from the seventies. If a soundtrack could be attached to a life, a place — muzak that works — it would be unmarketable with its odd diversity of tracks.

Nova adored her Saturdays in the Market and would fetch special coffees for Jorgé and herself as soon as the salon was prepared for the day. Busy days, he continually sent her on errands, so she had plenty of opportunities to enjoy the energy outside. The energy never failed to affect her, to lift her spirits. Saturdays felt as though she *had* joined the circus, when the vocals really came in from bullhorns held by communist workers, jam sessions in apartments, bars, or on the street. She grinned at the noise made by hawking fishmongers and the louder self-mongers and the Latin American orchestra dressed as charming peasants.

Underneath, like all markets, it possessed an ancient rhythmic hum created from trade, community, basic needs met, marriages — or at least couplings — made. This same music turns into white noise at a modern mall, some special secret element removed by its enclosure or the attempts at convenience. Kensington merchants laid down the basic beat with partial resistance to Sundays and evenings away from home: a foreign, decidedly un–North American beat. They ignored people who tried to bang the drum too hard, or directed them to the twenty-four-hour Dominion in the Annex.

◆

The salon closed Sundays and Mondays, so Nova was able to participate in the mercurial procession moving higgledy-piggledy through the streets. The purpose of their merry act of civil disobedience was to have the summer solstice re-declared a public holiday, and they handed out citrus-coloured invitations.

JUNE 21

CALL IN SICK
You are sick
SOLSTICE IS THE CURE
Make it a national holiday.

Tommy Gunn led the medieval pantomime with a series of leaps and twirls, dressed in obscenely tight bicycle shorts made barely decent with a flowing white pirate shirt. With a garland about his head to create a puckish persona, and a colourful xylophone tinging staccato bursts of sweetness, he attracted stares and occasional smiles. A Korean exchange student named Kim played a pan flute behind him, and Nova brought up the rear, shyly, with a little toy drum. Kim's target market was people of colour, while Nova's was her monied brethren. Tommy looked for the sad sacks, the difficult ones who appeared worn down and in need of extra attention, frequently pretty young women.

Tommy had written to his member of Parliament, his member of provincial Parliament, his city councillor, the mayor, the premier, and the prime minister, urging them all to recognize the sacred day. He'd suggested it be called Diana Day, if dead royalty was required before a holiday could be declared. Diana was the moon goddess, after all, and her more famous sister had died in the summer. As a footnote, he added other days that might become more appropriate and democratic holidays, the current ones being so Christian-centric and Anglo-centric, and therefore insulting to the Jews, the Muslims, Indians, Chinese, and every other group supposedly served by official multiculturalism. April Fool's, National Day of Mourning, Halloween, Each Person's Birthday, even Mother's and Father's Day, a concession to loathsome Hallmark holidays, were all certainly more worthy of proper restful celebration than the myth of some guy on a cross.

The procession turned into something of a pub crawl, with Tommy in the lead, and they invaded stores to create a ruckus. They collected a woman with the name Brigid from an aromatherapy store called Pagan Place, and Nova was put out when her position in line was usurped. The newcomer succeeded in ridding herself of all fifty of her invitations in the time it took Nova to unload five, because with her red hair, freckles, and overall Anne of Green Gables appearance, it was difficult to associate her with evil witches or subversion.

She told Nova about Brigid — or Bride, as she is known in Celtic mythology — fire goddess and patron of artists, smiths, and healers. A shrine to her in Kildare had been taken over by nuns after the Christianization of Ireland, and she became Saint Brigid, almost as important as the Virgin. This one had dancing eyes that drew Nova in. She wore her own skin so comfortably, seemed so completely at peace with herself and the world, that after an hour and two quick Bloody Marys, Nova's jealousy was replaced by respect, as though a spell had been cast.

They talked about how Christianity had usurped all the pagan festivals by placing their religious holidays around the originals. Some say Jesus was born in the summer, but the winter solstice fit in better with the story of sheltering God's son against the cold. Evergreens were appropriated and stripped of their symbolism of returning life, turned into totems to gift-giving. Easter has its fertility symbols in eggs and rabbits, the resurrection of a saviour fittingly implanted into a celebration of the life force. In placing their miracles and holidays near the pagan ones, the unholy were more easily converted. Everyone, after all, loves a party.

"They even stole the Virgin and raped her of her true virtue, her love of sexual pleasure. Our virgins had sex, they were pure in that they weren't married, were un-owned."

Nova had never thought a religion could celebrate sexuality and individuality. She'd viewed the procession as a whimsical bit of misbehaviour, having little to do with her own beliefs. But her wickedness would be excused under this faith, the way the Crusades were justified by Rome.

The next day, Nova helped Brigid collect donated food from merchants for an evening picnic in the park. She recognized about ten of the people at the celebration, Cerb and Lucky among them. They didn't recognize her, and she toyed with them for a while to test her anonymity. The moon came up full, and they watched it travel behind the tip of the tower in the southeast. It seemed to move at a great speed, and a general melancholy fell over the group as a result, the fact of passing time suddenly so apparent. Lucky became agitated and restless and was trying to convince Cerb to head over to the Greeks when a quartet of vested police officers arrived with flashlights to shine in their eyes, simply for the deer-in-headlights effect of it.

Brigid spoke to the men in a quiet, sultry voice, pointed out the glowing disc in the sky for their amazement, for justification of a group presence in a park. As they turned their heads, Lucky bolted. Cerb stuck out a foot in the path of the first officer to pursue his friend, and tripped him. The other three drew their batons and ordered the group to keep still. One went in the direction of Lucky, another made certain the tripped-up cop was unhurt, and the fourth put handcuffs on

Cerb. They ordered the remaining picnickers to stand and marshalled them to the back wall of the public toilets. There, they were searched and questioned.

"You have no right to do this," said Brigid. "We haven't done anything."

"Reasonable suspicion," said one of the cops.

"What's reasonable?" asked Brigid. "Sitting in a park? I think that's unreasonable."

The officers began questioning Nova, filling out what they called a contact report.

"You don't have to tell them squat, Nova," Brigid told her. "Identity cards were rejected a couple years ago as a violation of personal freedom."

But Nova was frightened. She felt her life as Nova should be recorded somewhere, that without it she could too easily disappear.

The officers checked on their car radios for past offences.

"You don't exist," they told her.

"Of course she exists," said Brigid. "She's standing right there, for Chrissake. Touch her, hear her, smell her."

"Nova Philip's my nickname," she said. "It's the only one I'll give you right now."

The following week held an officially sanctioned, don't-go-to-work holiday, because, apparently, the celebration of the natural universe is of less importance than the celebration of nation.

The bodies crammed in Tommy's tiny backyard formed a patchwork of age and colour. Nova stood in a corner and watched several punks, neon mohawks glowing in the bright

sun, as they tried to attach a Canadian flag to a rusty bad-
minton net pole. It kept slipping down, and each time it did
so they raced to prevent it from touching the ground in a
melodramatic show of patriotism. Everyone knew everyone
else, even Nova, if only from repeated sightings rather than
introductions, and Tommy was busy, playing with the children mostly, preferring their company to the adults'. When he
spotted her, he placed the child he was swinging like an air-
plane gently on the ground.

"Hi. I'm glad you came. Let me introduce you to some
people."

He led her by the hand towards a small group and suddenly stopped.

"Where's your beer, doll?"

"I didn't bring any."

"Well go and fetch one."

"Where?"

"There," and he pointed with pride towards a fridge with a
spout. "Two bucks for one. Five bucks for five."

"Five!"

"Yeah. A little inducement to buy a round."

He had it all figured out, he did, and she ordered five from
a tall Native standing behind a plywood counter. He wore a
seagull feather tucked into a red bandanna around his head as
a statement about the holiday. Nova told him she liked his
headdress and thought she might try to fashion one for herself.

She turned around and Tommy was there to relieve her of
two cups.

"I think those boys need to meet you. Gotta take a slash."

She walked tentatively to the pair he'd indicated: two
handsome boys with sinewy bodies and shadowed eyes.

"Hi. I'm Nova. These are for you, I guess."

"Thanks, Nova."

"No trouble."

"This is Bash. I'm Dino."

"Tommy's roommate. I like your art."

Dino wore a fifties newsman's hat with the word "shocking" torn from a headline and stuck in the band. She was about to ask him what was, when an ill-kept man loped down the alley to the yard. Dino excused himself, and she was inexplicably impressed when he drew a knife from the back of his jeans.

"Get out, you fuck. Don't be coming 'round here."

"I'm jonesing, man."

"I said, get out."

The man took a swing at Dino, but was stopped by a booted kick in the stomach. When he straightened up, Dino held the blade ready, unfolded and locked solid.

"Get the hell out of here. Can't you see there's children present?"

"Come on, Dino. I'm hurting. Just let me ask around."

"Didn't you hear me?"

"What's your problem, boy? You know the score."

Dino folded the knife and replaced it in his pocket. He turned to go, then smoothly pivoted and hit the intruder, square on the button, and strode into the house. The man picked himself up, scanned the crowd for an ally, and left.

Nova turned to Bash.

"What was that?"

"Market trash."

"Was he looking for drugs?"

Bash sneered at her. "Nah. He was looking for his ma."

Tommy and Dino came out then, pumped and puffed out

so they seemed bigger than before. Dino stuck his mouth over the tap of the beer fridge and Tommy pulled the lever. Nova finished her glass and went for a refill.

"Are you okay?" she asked Dino.

"Yeah, man. Guy didn't touch me."

"Good thing," said Tommy. "I would've kicked his skinny junkie ass back to Vancouver, where it belongs."

"Why not call the police?" she asked.

"We take care of our own problems here."

"What about the night I met you?"

"That was different," Tommy said.

"How?"

"Those people were outsiders. Unfortunately, that piece of shit lives here now. He may be a freak and the worst kind of junkie, but he's a neighbour. We have our own ways of dealing with them."

"What about law and order?"

"I told you already. No one obeys the law around here. We have our own, internal order."

"What, you really just do as you please? Assault people you don't like?"

Tommy looked to Dino for an explanation of the obvious waste of skin before him. Dino touched the brim of his hat in answer and walked away.

"Those are Market rules. If you can't dig them, go back to your husband and your pretty little life."

"God, you really can be such an asshole, can't you."

"Go polish your face, schoolgirl."

Seething at Tommy, Nova joined a group of women from the Plate, Collette and the purple-haired woman among them. They laughed at her, gave her advice about not taking Market boys too seriously. These ladies moved from one man to another and somehow managed to all stay friends in the end. "Serial endogamy," said a woman who studied anthropology as a hobby. What else are you going to do? Move away? No relationship was that important, really, not if you had entwined circles of friends and wished to remain part of the community.

Nova tried to imagine a swinging door among the bedrooms of her past life. It was so sacred, monogamy and till death us do part, unquestioned in theory if not in actual practice. These women just laughed about their latest failed romances and carried on and seemed happy and miraculously in control of their lives. They chatted frankly about fights and drinking in alleys, and Nova felt a bit like a Mary Poppins. These women wore halter tops and allowed their less-than-firm bellies to show; they spoke openly of their shortcomings and didn't allow them to affect their lives. For this, Nova had to give them credit. They had grown children who sometimes came around for a drink with their moms. Exes came around with new wives and stepkids, and they all tumbled into the same collective family as though they really were a tribe.

One of them had a spliff and Nova took several deep tokes. She giggled about the significance of this Canada Day and how much better it was than any Fourth of July party she'd ever attended. Last year it had been a catered company picnic with mandatory participation in three-legged races for employees, and a men-only tug-of-war. Team-building, it was, rather than a holiday. No alcohol. Lots of children on display, and wives sitting off to the side in the shade.

Tommy sauntered over to offer up a back-handed apology, and the conflicting plaids of his shirt and shorts seemed quite hilarious to her. He asked if she needed a walk home, but she waved him off.

"I'm Mary Poppins," she giggled, "and I can fly there with my umbrella if the wind changes."

"Watch her," he told Collette. "She might try to jump into some pavement art."

There was another party to go to, an annual birthday bash of a retired lounge singer who lived in the equivalent of a Market suburb, the interior, a little enclave down an alley and off the main streets. She'd hooked up a sound system, and anyone who so desired could step up to the mike. In the backyard, other musicians sat around and strummed guitars and sang sixties songs that everyone knew the words to. Even Nova knew a few of them, the famous Neil Youngs and Joni Mitchells. One of the women told Nova that Joni had given up a daughter and that daughter had been a Market regular until one day she did one of those searches and came up with Joni.

They ate potato salad and cheese and bread and Genoa salami, and, once fortified, moved on, crashed another party because the music filtered down onto Fish Street and grabbed them, and everyone else had run out of beer. Film students were having a show, projecting their final projects through the window and onto the wall of the new Kensington lofts across the road.

The images sputtered and bounced erratically on the makeshift screen, making Nova dizzy to the point that she feared she'd crash through the window. Without a word, because she really couldn't have formed one if she'd wanted to, she rappelled down the stairs and out to the street for air.

She walked slowly through the sky. It had descended to

the pavement and was no longer just black air to trap smells, to breathe. She searched for stars at eye level, but only moons dotted the length of the street, each perfectly full and undisturbed by cloud cover. A density in the atmosphere slowed her movement, caused resistance and exhaustion. She thought about crawling, wished she were a cat with four legs to take her to bed.

Her keys had been switched with someone else's, for the one she tried to insert in the lock wouldn't fit. The hole was old-fashioned and large. She didn't remember her key being old-fashioned. Skeleton key. That was the kind, on a big brass loop she never had. She took a few steps away from the door to assess the whole. It was most definitely her house. Not her key. It was such a beautiful night, with so many moons and the sky descended to the pavement, that it made sense to sleep outside in it.

◆

Although it was the most pain she'd ever known, her initial reaction was analytical, to wonder what it was. It didn't entirely knock her out of her stupor. Opening her eyes to the sight of him alerted her primal instincts, and they completed the job. She curled in a ball to protect her organs and found some words to whisper, as though a whisper was an appropriate response. When she produced a scant five dollars, she was kicked again, in the head, skull against brick. The sky retreated to its proper place.

May 31

"Are you still taking your pills?"

Christ, he knows how to start a morning. Does he actually believe they are lobotomizing?

"It's not the pills, Brendan. In fact, I took two yesterday, so I should've been sweet as saccharine. I don't like all these surprises sprung on me."

"But it's great news, princess. I didn't think I'd make partner for another five years."

"I know it's great. I'm happy for you, really."

I guess I don't look convinced, so he comes and kisses my cheek.

"Work will be good for you too."

Before he leaves, he gives me the card to get myself some appropriate partner's wife clothing. Where did I see that graffiti, the words scrawled in oxymoronic red lipstick on a bathroom wall: "I could have been a trophy wife"? The author had been extremely drunk, by the look of the handwriting, and I initially read it as "atrophy." Here I am. The hotter the wife, the more successful the man. Not too flash, tastefully flash. Works the same way with the secretaries. I learned that when I worked at the firm too. Partners have these gorgeous babes working for them as executive assistants, really styling; and don't kid yourself, they're well paid for it, paid to look fine. The ugly ones — married or ugly — never worked for a man higher up than senior consultant, or worked for women, but that was sort of the same thing. There weren't any female partners then, must be now.

Married EAs must be professionally attired. With a little help from a few fashion magazines, I get a sense of what's in this year. Pencil skirts below the knee, grey anything, white shirts. Not for the first time in my life, I wonder what today's women would be were it not for these mags? More or less confident without the visible uniformity of fashion? Fat and frumpy without glamorous ideals to live up to? Wealthy from the money saved by wearing clothes till they fall apart or poor from never having the motivation to earn enough to acquire all the seasonal must-haves? I take my pill so I won't make decisions based on depression.

Holt's has a doorman to welcome me, to make me feel special and privileged from the moment I enter. All the fragrance counters are right at the front so it smells decadent and feminine as well.

The racks are filled with some of the best clothes in the world, all silky, or cashmere soft, fabrics chosen to look expensive, feel delicate, and last a single season. Some of the pieces I try on are likely to disintegrate with the slightest exertion on my part, and these are the items I choose. I tell the hovering woman the look I'm meant to achieve, and she knows it so perfectly, is so adept and thoughtful of the process, that I'm tempted to ask her if she'd like to go and take my place. She steers me away from bright colours and young avant-garde designers.

There's a spa in the store, and on a whim I book a session. Hair, facial, massage. For three hours I'm cosseted and rubbed with unguents and revitalizing creams. The masseuse spends a long time on the flaccid muscles of my inner thighs and buttocks. I try to think sad thoughts to prevent arousal, to save myself from the primal urge to just roll over and give myself up to those well-trained hands. My eyebrows are plucked, a few nose hairs removed, the pain eye-watering. It's followed by a delicate face massage to ease the tension, steam cleaning, warm mud wrap. They do the hair last. Fingertips stimulate my scalp during a wash, and the stylist gently rubs my shoulders while we discuss my hair. I tell him I want to be sexy but more sophisticated, a little less suburban in appearance.

It's not bad, this free-fall shopping, with personable, attractive, young salesclerks telling me how great I look, sincere compliments. The nicer they are, the more I want to buy from them, give them commissions. Some places you know the women are lying, can see with your own eyes that the garment makes you appear dowdy, is poorly stitched, the wrong colour, or too large a pattern. But they go on and on about how it suits you, say their tailor will fix the flawed workmanship, alter the top always made for a bustier woman, the length. It's an American Express card inserted in my wallet, so I don't even have to concern myself with a limit. I'm not checking prices, just getting what I want, novelty and the promise of adventure. Leather jacket from the Beaver store, soft, tasteful, with only the faintest suggestion of a biker, just enough to make me feel a little trendy. New jeans, a size larger, and baggy khakis good for swing dancing if I ever get the urge. I'm covering all the potential bases: dinners at good restaurants, weekends away at more cottages, home entertaining outfits. I get two suits for work and complete my day with an impulse buy of a whimsical green scarf draped nicely near a register.

That evening, I give Brendan a fashion show, complete with music. He approves of everything but the scarf, asks if I'm trying to be Amelia Earhart or something. I laugh at the minor criticism and finish the display by stripping to show him the sexy new girdle that pushes everything up or into its proper position.

◆

I need to take advantage of my final days of freedom and I have to expand more than my wardrobe for the job at hand. I must expand my mind, my knowledge, become more cultured and less of a philistine. Now there's a fitting phil word for the day. Philis. She decides on the shoe museum as the appropriate first step towards enlightenment. She can work herself up to more serious cultural pursuits.

The building itself resembles a shoe box. So clever. Inside, Philis learns the historical, sociological, and anthropological significance of footwear. Who knew shoes were so historical and significant? Perhaps my fetish for such accessories is not so frivolous after all, perhaps it's an inherent, evolved need. After the experience, I'm so impressed with all I've learned that I stop at Town Shoes and add a pair of artifacts to my collection.

◆

The streets surrounding the Art Gallery of Ontario are completely uninspired, unaffected by the brilliance contained within the massive concrete structure. The creative energy inside hasn't managed to seep out and expand, has not infected the street, apart from two sculptures placed strategically to help identify the stark, characterless building as a home of art.

Instead, that section of Dundas Street is lined with uninteresting restaurants, a chain coffee shop on one corner, and its mercantile equivalent, a dollar store, on the other, offering cheap disposable crap. The Ontario College of Art and Design cozies up beside the gallery, but even its art students have not been motivated to affect their environment, not even with graffiti or the establishment of a place to hang out. Where is the energy people bring out of there? Perhaps they hoard it, keep it close around them, the experience used only to make themselves more interesting to others. Isn't that what I'm doing?

Two blocks north it improves, but tree-lined Baldwin Street — Baldwin Village, it's called — is definitely separate from the gallery, existing in defiance of its neighbour. It's a tiny oasis of lazy Mediterranean attitude, with people enjoying late afternoon lunches outside. There's even a picnic table in front of a Chinese bakery, and I can't remember the last time I sat at a picnic table. Inside, I look at the items available in a display case and can't decide which one I want. In the name of culinary experimentation rather than gluttony, I ask for a curried beef bun, deep-fried pork roll, vegetarian spring roll, and an almond cookie. The food is enhanced by the experience of the picnic table, as though it is a rare and priceless condiment, like the secret spice added to a simple sandwich prepared by someone who loves you.

The sticky rice surrounding a dollop of pork mixture is a sweet, glutinous blob more like a dessert than a savory snack. I could live on these, likely a million calories but who cares. My cares and worries have no place on this street where harried faces, honking horns, and self-importance are absent. The very air feels different as it stirs the leaves, the branches acting as a metronome to conduct the tempo of life, a natural cue to slow down. If only Brendan could experience this. But it's not possible, is it, for him. He'd never sit here and wonder who these people are with freedom of time on a Wednesday afternoon.

The street signs aren't misleading, it does feel like a village, an authentically global one. There's a Mexican restaurant, an Italian café, a couple of French bistros, a Middle-Eastern place, this Chinese bakery, a Thai restaurant, and a shop selling Indonesian imports. For the first time, I get an idea of the potential of this city of immigrants.

◆

The next day, I awake early with a longing for another excursion. I recall Pasquale and his suggestions, think a market might be right.

As I turn onto Kensington Avenue, I experience the strangest sense of déjà vu, an odd sensation of truly coming home. Victorian houses, tarted up beyond their era in bold primary colours, now sell vintage clothing. They've all left their racks outside in the drizzling rain, and though they're covered with plastic tarpaulins, the dampness has seeped in so the musty smell of dirty old clothes seeps out and perfumes the street. Ma used to dry my wet mittens and socks on the living room rad in the winter, and the whole house smelled like this.

I go into food shops where they immediately ask if I want to taste something, a morsel of bread at the bakery, smoked chèvre from a cheese shop. At a Portuguese store, a tray of custard tarts has just come out of the oven, and the missus gives me one. It's like a little taste of sweet warm love, and I am so grateful I buy six of them.

I pick up a quart of strawberries as a treat for Brendan. He's been talking about Ontario strawberries, seducing me with descriptions of their red juiciness, claiming Californian ones are tasteless in comparison. They do look redder and fatter than any I've ever seen.

There's a café on the corner, off the beaten track, clean and organic looking, unlike the others I've passed. My instincts about the place are slightly off, though. I can't smoke, and earnest young student types look at me in my expensive new clothes as if I'm some sort of freak show.

Someone has left the city's tabloid on a table, and I flip through it so I won't seem like such a loser, here, on my own, obviously not belonging.

Reading the brief items on bestiality, child abuse, and kiddie-porn rings, armed robbery of East Indian or Korean corner stores, I discover how easy it has been to isolate myself from the unseemly aspects of my new city. By sticking to the staid national daily, I might assume that crime happens else-where, that standing on guard for thee has actually worked.

The crime-stopper column provides readers with an oppor-tunity to help control the encroaching urban violence and make a few bucks while doing so. An abortionist has been shot somewhere back home, but I don't read the details. I want to read only the most outrageous examples of malignant human behaviour, the chronicles of reality ignored in my quest for a preferred existence. I want to be reassured that my life is better now.

◆

The electricity in the air makes the cats skittish and they roam about everywhere. Animals sense the onset of severe weather, don't they? Earthquakes and such? They know it's coming hours in advance and get all freaky. Probably people do too, but don't recognize what's affecting them, like craziness at the full moon. It's easier to measure behaviour during the full moon, though, because it's charted and visible. I try to smell the electricity, but it's hidden under the blanket of market odours.

I can see the storm moving in from the west, black sky just over an incinerator tower. Thunder cracks loudly and rumbles on and the wind whips up the garbage in the street, giving it a film noir atmosphere. There are two tentative drops of warning before the rain comes down in a sheet, more tropical than Canadian.

I'm soaking wet from the downpour and can barely walk in my shoes, the way my feet keep sliding forward out the open bits. They'll be ruined, and I'd take them off if I could get away with it. Not only is the sidewalk likely swarming with bacteria and viruses, but shards of glass could be anywhere. I run/hobble to a restaurant and sit under an awning to watch the God show.

The rain smells sad, smells like the funerals I've been to, always in the rain. "God's tears," said Da. "God's confetti," he told me on my wedding day. Farmers and seamen can smell its approach, and I wonder what it is they sense, what molecules precede the drops. Suddenly, the temperature plunges and pellets of hail bounce off the concrete of the patio. I use the opportunity to go inside to get a beer, and the ice stings my scalp and exposed limbs.

People stand in doorways to watch. I think a thunderstorm is one of the only ways to really experience nature in the city, to have it surround and show off. Its anger is a way to summon attention, like a scorned lover acting out his rage. This storm does not call forth Mother Nature in a white flowy gown. These are Olympian gods at play.

A young squeegee girl runs up the street looking for shelter, sees how the awning protects me, and darts in.

"Wow. I missed got hit by the lightning."

She sounds French and is striking. She's beautiful, even trying to look ugly or tough, or whatever appearance they attempt to achieve. She reeks of patchouli oil masking body odour and the peculiar goatlike smell of unwashed hair. I'd have expected such a fresh shade of green to smell of peppermint, maybe, or cut grass. But even in her filthy and odiferous state, she has more finesse than I do, and I'm instantly jealous of her for that. We have similar features, and I try to imagine how I would feel and act if we were able to change skins. We start talking about how we wound up in Toronto and eventually I sit back and just listen and nod every now and then, because I find her fascinating.

◆

It was a very good trip. We had a pound of marijuana. Very good trip, that. But I think it made me crazy. The marijuana. Bogotá. Colombia. It is worse than in your movies.

I went home after six months and was fucked in the head. I went to a psychiatrist. My parents were very afraid and wanted me to live in their house. I asked them for a few francs for food, and they said if I want to eat, come to their table. Their food was rotten to me. I only wanted a little of my own. In France, it is law. Parents must provide for their children, even if they are not in the same house.

My mother cried every time she saw me. She was really crazy. Bad trip. I told her she had no right. I told her thousands of women now work in France. She has never worked a day in her life. She doesn't even clean her own house. If I am there, I clean it. How can she say I am wasting my life?

I was even skinnier than now. And white. My father is big researcher in SIDA. I tried heroin in Bogotá. Very good trip. But I kept worrying about him. So only marijuana. Do you like heroin? Really. You should. Once. To know.

So then I come to Canada.

My mother and my sister want me to stop moving around. I tell them I have my whole life to stop moving. My sister, I love. She has a baby and I adore him. He is gorgeous. She came to see where I was living. It was a squat. She was upset because there were — how do you say it in English — the hair, like this. Punks. Yes. And there were many drugs. But I tell her not to say my address to my parents. And she didn't. That is why I love her.

When I first came here, I was sleeping in the streets. I had a sleeping bag, so I was warm. It was okay. Then some fuck stole it, but it was warmer, so I didn't need it. Now I am staying in my friend Lucas's flat. He saved my life, I think, so I love him. No, it is more than love. Do you know that feeling? Too bad.

You know, in Bogotá, they shoot children in the street. Yes, like dogs. The police say they want for it to be safe for tourists. No tourists in Bogotá. The drug dealers shoot them also. There was one boy, only four years old, who I kept trying to get to come stay with me. He said he was safe, that they wouldn't shoot someone so young. I found him one morning. A small bullet, here. I buried him all alone. Myself. That is when I was crazy and went to Paris.

May I have a cigarette? Here, this one is broken. I was able to fix them when I was younger. Twenty-six. You?

I can't stand it now when people say they have this problem or that problem. I get angry with them.

Do you have a boyfriend? Really? I'll never do that. I like men too much. I like them better than women. You cannot say fuck to women. He is a really good fuck. No, they say, not fuck, make love. Yes, maybe they don't. I do.

When I was living on the street, a man tried to rape me. I told him, I have a knife and I will stab you, but he didn't believe me. I stabbed him and phoned the police and told them there is a man here, laying in his own blood, and this girl won't be here when you get here. The papers report it. They're looking for me, so I think I'll go now. Maybe to India.

Do you think I was wrong? He died. But I think it's okay that he died. Sometimes we must kill, no? Good. It's survival, I think. Have you ever killed anything? No, don't cry. Oh, I'm sorry. It's not that bad. In France, we have a little pill so it just goes away. Very sophisticated, I think. None of your sadness or shame.

There. Rain stops and so I go. Rain is good for the work, yes? Ciao.

◆

She left a pall of patchouli in her place. I keep swallowing to prevent the vomit from filling my mouth.

In the alley beside the restaurant, I let it out and brace myself against the wall. The spot reeks of garbage and urine and previous puke, and as I stand there trying to collect myself, I know these smells will forever remind me of choice. I look at a wall painted with pretty Bavarian castles and puke again.

◆

The paper becomes a full-scale addiction and I read every article involving Toronto crime. My adrenaline pumps as I hand change to the store clerk, as I carry the newspaper to the coffee shop to read. I keep it from Brendan, don't mention the tawdry and heinous acts, don't report on my keen interest in the news. I search for information about the girl and for the tidbits of reality from which I have withdrawn. Reading the paper is ritualized. The articles are clipped and pasted in a school notebook, the atrocity file, I call it.

There are definitely bad areas of town, but all parts of the city have interesting crimes going on, and I paste them in to remind me that no place is safe, no one immune or perfect. A dwarf and the owner of a circus school have been accused of raping the proprietor's ex-wife in a suburban neighbourhood. One of the two took photos. The item leaves it to the reader's imagination to speculate on who did what, which would make the better picture, and for what purpose, what sort of mind.

A pair of women arrested for stabbing a cop and killing him are described as fat, as though that had as much bearing on their guilt as racist sentiments no longer acceptable to print. The next day, amid snatches of eulogies from a carnival funeral, the newspaper reports on what the two tubs of lard ate throughout their first day of incarceration. It causes me to wonder who cared. What sort of person wants to laugh at fat female cop killers pigging out on prison food?

Someone is killed in that laneway beside Hemingway's, and the people of Yorkville are outraged that it happened in their backyard. Others are outraged that access to their hair-dressers is denied by the yellow crime-scene tape proclaiming do not cross.

I am trying to "mise en place" these incidents. If I can be aware of them, but keep them safely pasted in my book, I can control them, prevent them from creeping into my life.

I can convince myself that I'm not a bad person for killing my baby, like that girl cannot be judged wrong for protecting herself. But she would be, and so would I by other standards. It was such a relief to tell someone and not be judged, and I wish I could tell Ma or Da or Brendan. But that's impossible.

His voice startles me, hollering from the foyer. I hide the notebook under the bed and dart into the bathroom to turn on the shower. The water smells slightly earthy, and I feel unclean, scurfy, and sticky, so scrub my skin with a loofah. I pull on a pair of stretch pants and one of Brendan's tee-shirts.

"Where'd you park the trailer?"

"What?"

"You look like someone who lives in a trailer park."

"So?"

"We're going to look at houses. You have to change."

I strip off the tee-shirt and throw it at him. The pants too.

"What should I wear?"

What is it that suddenly turns him on? The nudity created as a result of his demands? The edge of anger in the air? His thought that I'm a lesser being because of my wardrobe choice? I fuck him like I hate him, like I'm beating him, and he responds in kind.

"Wow," he says afterwards. "That was amazing."

◆

I'm not prepared to embed myself like this, to stick down roots. It feels almost as confining as having children.

"We're wasting our time renting, Phillie. Not to mention the money. It makes no sense to just give that money to someone else."

"I know," I say, feeling strangled. "But Andrews could transfer you back to Cincinnati."

"They're not going to transfer me. Once they make you a partner, it's up to you. You bid for the locations, not the other way around. I'd have to put in for Cincinnati, and frankly, I'd rather stay here. I thought we sorted that out."

I look out the window rather than respond and can feel him looking at me for confirmation.

"I bet once you see what we can buy here, you'll change your mind."

I'd like a big cave in which to hibernate from the world. I'm lost in my head, stupidly imagining how one could decorate a cave, when Brendan says, "Oh, Christ." I look at him and see her, and don't know how to react. Brendan rolls down his window far enough to yell at her. I want to stop him but my voice is frozen. The window goes up and I stare straight ahead. The girl looks me square in the eye and gives me the finger, shouts something we can't hear.

"God, they're obnoxious. Look at her. Green hair. So many holes in her head she probably leaks. When we have kids, Phillie, promise me they won't turn out like that."

"I talked to her the other day," I whisper. "She's really quite bright."

"If she's so bright, what's she doing cleaning windshields for a living?"

"She's chosen that lifestyle. She ran away from home."

"Someone ought to just round them all up and take them over to Africa or somewhere, give them a reason to be grateful for their privilege."

◆

The first house we view smells of cat piss from a litter box that hasn't been changed in weeks, it seems. It's difficult to concentrate on the positive features with the ammonia making my eyes water. To make things worse, someone burned incense to try to mask it, and the combination of smells is confusing to me. I crinkle my nose at Brendan, who nods and hurries the real estate agent through. He doesn't even try to be polite about it, and when we're finally outside Brendan tells him he must be insane to think he can sell a hole like that for more than a quarter of a million dollars. He laughs and tells us he knows he can.

The odours in the second house are different, stacked individually in the air like a parfait of the past few meals: fried eggs and bacon for breakfast, curry last night, and perhaps fish the day before. I can taste it, it's so strong. The dump of a backyard is filled with bicycle parts and broken furniture and a week's worth of garbage. Bile rises and I swallow, my memory making its connection.

When we enter the third place for sale, it's like stepping into the pages of *Better Homes and Gardens*, complete with scent strips of cozy rooms. The owner must have just baked something and then left, and when we go into the kitchen I expect to find an apple pie set out for us. Each meticulously decorated room has a scent to give it a false sense of warmth: roses blooming in the living room from a bowl of potpourri; green apple soap in the guest toilet; sleepy sheets in the bedroom, the freshly laundered smell that makes me crave naps. Even in the nursery, I can detect talcum, untainted by dirty diapers.

"That was better," says Brendan back in the car. "Don't you think?"

"It didn't seem quite right. It didn't feel like anyone real lives there."

"It's an old real estate agent trick. Put cinnamon on the burner for a couple of minutes to make a place seem homey."

I think back to the previous homes.

"How can a place smell repulsive and welcoming at the same time?"

"What do you mean?"

"The first two houses. Didn't you notice? They smelled of life, whereas the last one seemed so confining."

"They just smelled is all. There was nothing welcoming about them."

July 4

I can't remember what he looked like. He has no face, no colour, no shape, only smell: like maggots, as though he was rotting and crawling with them. I need to put perfume there, under my nose, to get rid of it. It's deeper than that, it's inside. It's best to sleep. Dreams don't smell.

Tommy is here, holding my hand. He is crying in his strange way, and I tell him not to. I scream it at him because it frightens me.

Brendan is here. He's saying he doesn't know me. He's calling me names and demanding the police. I try to tell him, but the words won't work properly.

Tommy brings a picture of a pretty place. A bunch of poodles. He asks the nurse for morphine. She refuses. No drugs for trauma patients. No drugs for green-haired women found beaten in Kensington Market. Junkies will do just about anything for a fix. How do we know she isn't simply after morphine? Tommy holds out my arm and the nurse shrugs.

The smell disappears and I smile vaguely. He climbs into bed and holds me tightly against him and I sleep.

I wake up crying and he gives me another tablet. He strokes my head, rocks me gently back.

In my dream, I am naked and dancing alone, slowly, to the beat of my heart. I lie down and believe it is the world, not the clouds, that is moving so quickly. I am driving the world, and all I must do is say stop, and it will. But I can't find the word and the world moves faster. I must press myself into the dirt to keep from being flung into the sky and scream the word. I awaken as I fall off, and do not know where I am.

The noise summons a nurse.

"Are you all right?"

"I think so, yes. How long have I been here?"

"Two days."

"Jesus."

"You're not hurt. A little bruised, but you'll be fine. I'll get the doctor now."

I lean back and breathe, memory coming back in flashes. The crowded yard. Going into the corner to smoke a joint so we wouldn't have to share with too many people.

"Hi, I'm Dr. Small. You're back in the land of the living are you?"

"Afraid so."

"Do you remember what happened to you?"

"Sort of."

"I see. Were you on something?"

"I was quite drunk and too high, yes."

"Is there someone you'd like us to call to come and get you?"

"Can I have some time to think about it?"

"This is a busy hospital, missy. We have to release you in the morning. Do you have somewhere to stay? There are women's shelters available."

"No. I have a place to stay."

"Okay. You'll have to make a statement to the police."

"I don't want to talk to the police." I'm thinking of rules and order, trying to sort out what I believe in my addled head. What I want.

"You have no choice. They want to talk to you."

◆

I'm still groggy from whatever it is Tommy's been giving me, so when the police ask me where my home is, I hesitate because I don't know what to tell them. I think there must be a right answer and a wrong one, but the worst one is the sort of delayed response I provide. They ask me where I got the purse I had with me, and it confuses me. I tell them I think it was at Saks but it could have been Target, and I don't understand why they care. They think this is an insolent joke, and I realize what they mean and that 1000 Avenue Road is the right address to provide. I'm still too tired to be angry that they are more concerned with the bag than with the fact that I'm here, in a hospital, hurt.

They've already telephoned Mrs. Donahue, they say. She's on her way to pick it up. I know they're lying because I'm right here, don't know why they're trying to trick me, and I tell them that's impossible. They tell me Mr. Donahue wants to know where his wife is, and I suggest they look closely at the passport photo, ask them to quiz me on any of the stats on the ID. They are apparently disappointed that I pass this test and sort of toss the bag into my lap. They hand me the passport, and I look at the picture of a young woman with dead green eyes.

"You're Mrs. Philippa Maria Donahue?"

"I'm Phillie," I say. "I live above a store called Asylum, in Kensington Market."

Acknowledgments

Editorial: Marnie Kramarich and Don Bastian at Stoddart for patiently guiding my manuscript. Jonathan Bennett, Dominic Farrell, Wendy Morgan, The Elite Book Club, and Suzanne Brandreth and David Johnston at Livingston Cooke for their advice.

Housing: Jennifer Arklay for selflessly giving up her room just because. Lisa Malarz for the trout farm. Eithne McCredie and Robert Wilson for their third floor. Ramona MacRae for the time at Markham Street. Lascelle Wingate and Pat Bradley for the month of breathing space.

Transportation: Gillian Grant and Gord Potts for the Volvo. Peter Lightfoot for the Wolverine.

Technical: The service department at CPUsed for continuing to repair archaic equipment.

And finally, all the people in Kensington Market who keep me laughing and sane.